TO MY FAMILY,
ESPECIALLY MY MOTHER
WHO FUNDED MY "KUNG FU SAN SOO"
CLASSES WHEN I WAS IN JUNIOR HIGH.
IF ONLY IT HAD BEEN KARATE,
I WOULD BE A NINJA WARRIOR BY NOW!

(JUST JOKING, MOM!)

—D.J. MILKY

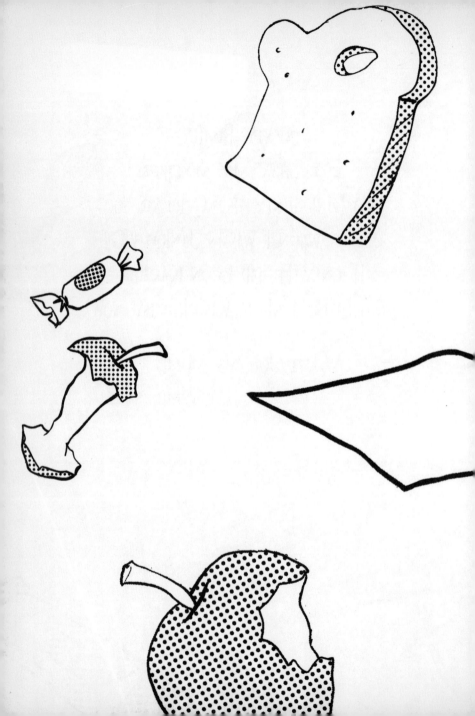

Contents

CHAPTER ONE

MEET MARVIN

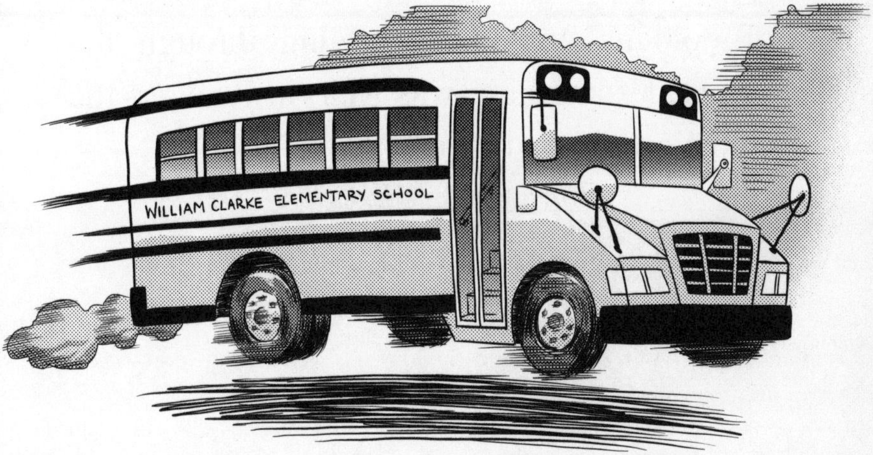
WILLIAM CLARKE ELEMENTARY SCHOOL

A big yellow bus screeched to a stop outside William Clarke Elementary School. The air filled with giggles and chatter as the kids filed out of the bus and up the stairs at school. Then all was silent.

But just before the bus driver slammed the door, something came tumbling down the steps. It sounded like rolling thunder and looked like a whirling backpack with legs. It crash-landed on the sidewalk, sending books, apple cores, candy wrappers, and even slices of bologna and cheese flying through the air. That something was Marvin Klutzer, the clumsiest third-grader around.

A timid voice called out, "Are you okay, Marvin?" The voice belonged to Ulysses Rodriguez. He was Marvin's best-ever friend. He was a year younger, and he looked up to Marvin like a big brother. Other kids called them nerds, dorks, even mega-geekazoids. But Marvin and Ulysses were friends to the end.

"Yep, fine. It was an accident," Marvin said, brushing himself off. "No biggie."

Maybe it wasn't a biggie to Marvin, but everyone else always thought it was funny when Marvin tripped over his own feet. They all laughed when he stepped into George the janitor's bucket of soapy water. And they howled when he somehow managed to get his head stuck in the toilet. "Klutzer the Clumsy Klutz" was always fumbling into something.

"Maybe you should have tied your shoelaces," whispered Ulysses, pointing at Marvin's feet.

"I know how to tie my shoes," said Marvin. "But I was way too busy today to deal with it. Besides, wearing untied shoes is *way* cooler. Soon all my fans will be doing it . . ."

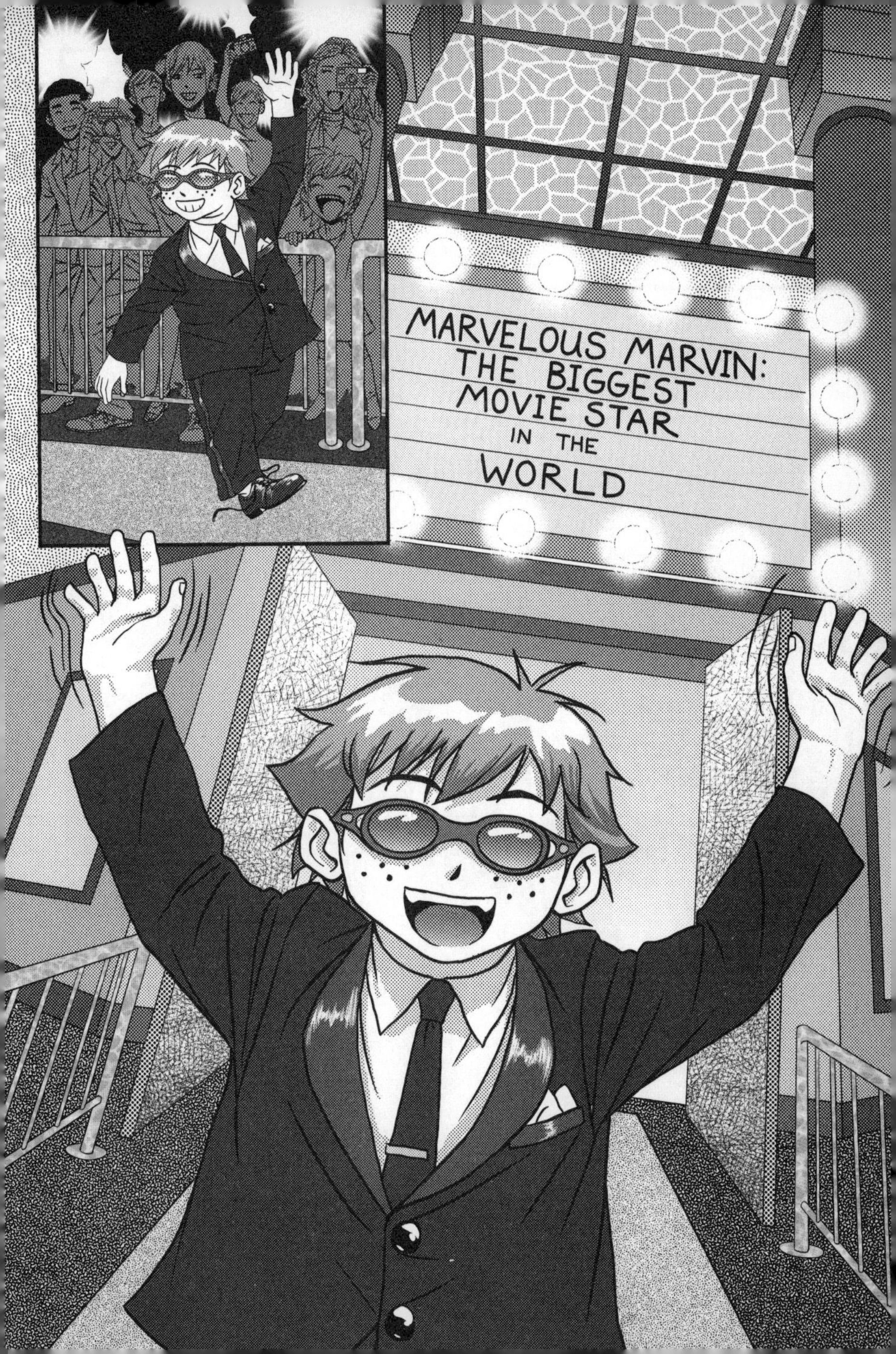
MARVELOUS MARVIN:
THE BIGGEST
MOVIE STAR
IN THE
WORLD

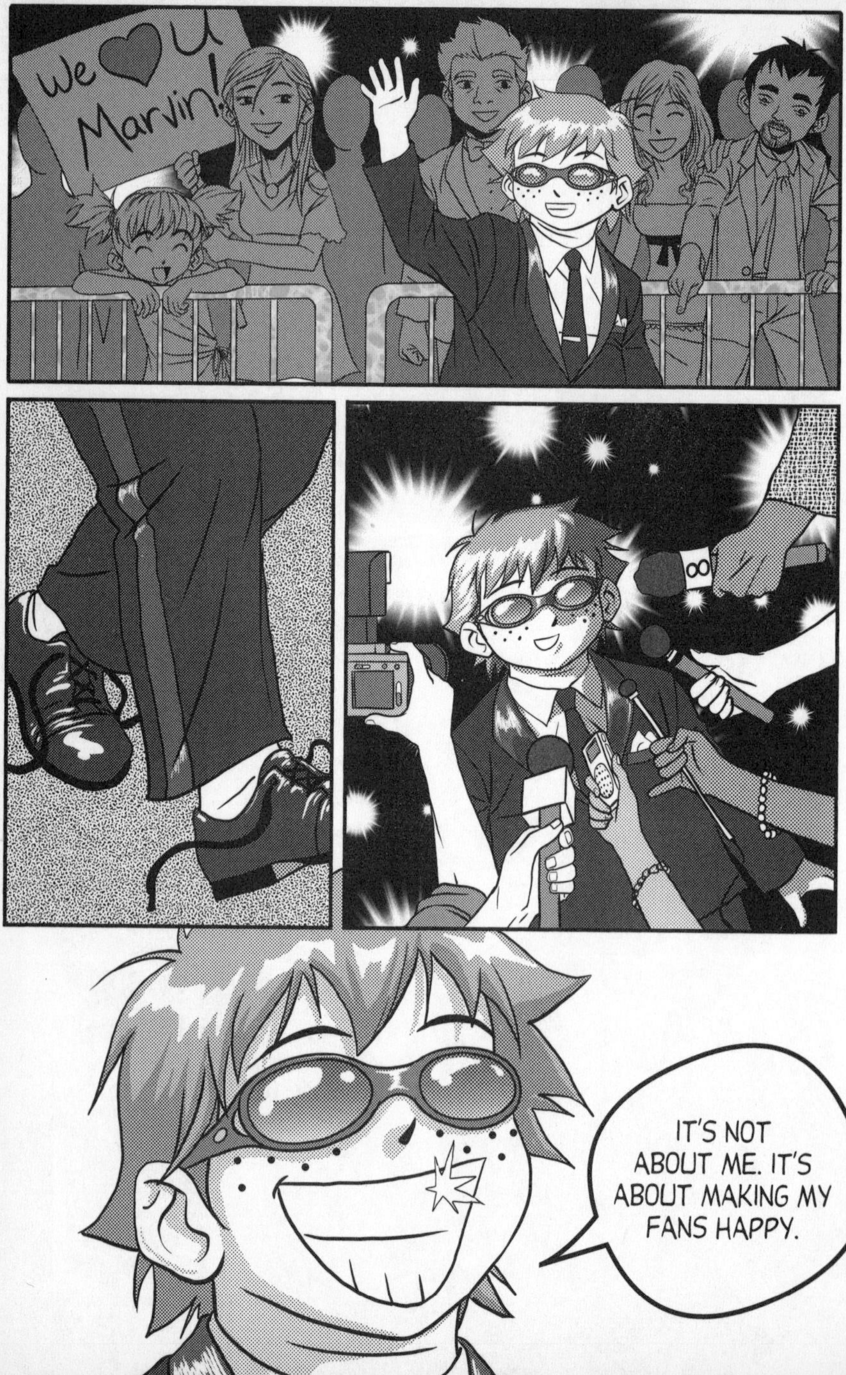

We ♥ U Marvin!
IT'S NOT ABOUT ME. IT'S ABOUT MAKING MY FANS HAPPY.

But what was really happening was not as marvelous as what Marvin had imagined.

"Cool threads!" snickered a girl.

"Nice view!" shouted a boy.

Marvin was mystified. "What's everyone looking at?"

And then he looked down. His pants had fallen to his ankles, and everyone could see his underwear!

Marvin quickly pulled up his pants. He had been in such a hurry to catch the bus that he didn't just forget to tie his shoes—he also forgot to wear a belt!

"Uh, no biggie," he muttered, scrambling into the building. All he wanted to do was get to class before anything else happened.

But standing in the hallway was Marvin's worst nightmare: Henry "Hank" Howell. Hank was a year older than Marvin and at least a head taller. He was big, he was cool, and he was really really mean.

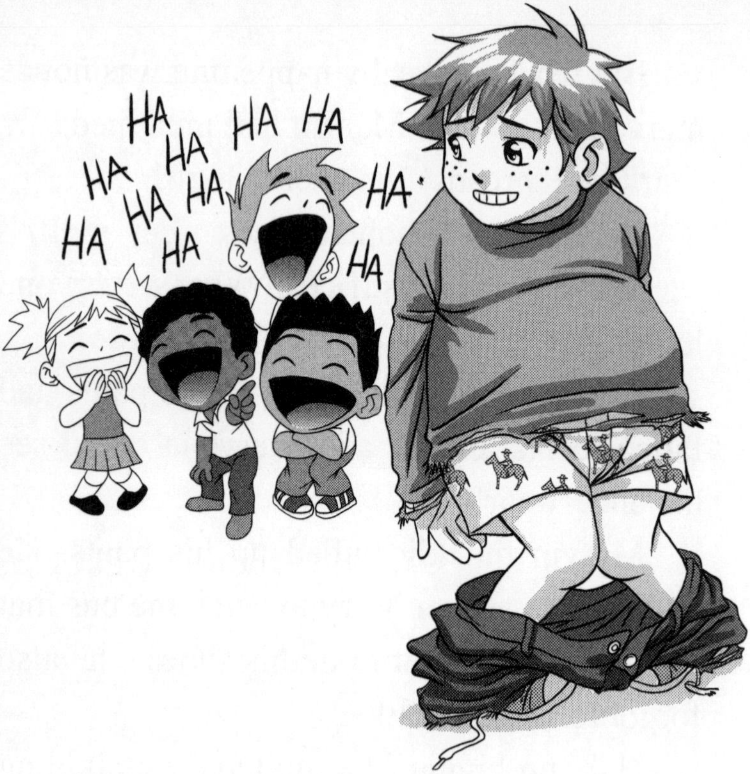
HA
HA
HA HA
HA
HA HA
HA
HA
HA
HA HA
HA

Hank enjoyed doing one thing more than anything else. He loved to pick on kids who were smaller than him. And who was more fun to push around than klutzy Marvin Klutzer?

Hank was never without his two loyal buds: Scratch and Sniff. Scratch's real name was Jeffrey, but he was always scratching himself. He said it was a "skin condition," from the dry weather, but who knows what that actually meant.

And no one could remember Sniff's real name, but he constantly had a cold and never stopped wiping his drippy nose. So, Sniff it was.

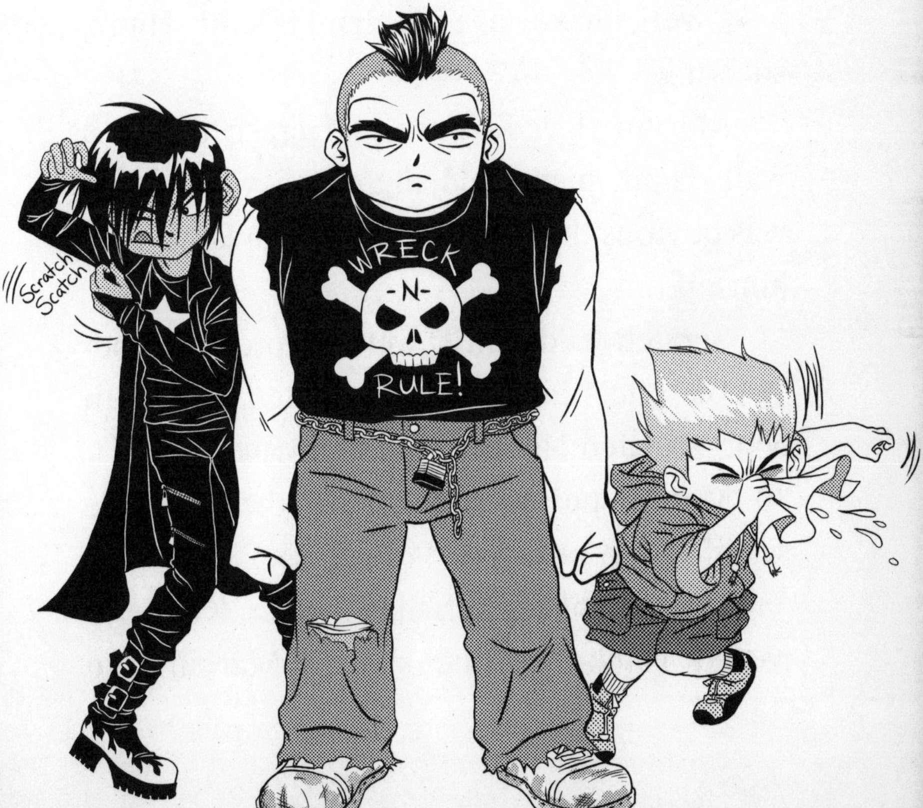
Scratch
Scatch
WRECK
-N-
RULE!

Marvin called them the Terrible Trio.

"Yo, Klutzer!" shouted Hank, blocking Marvin's path. "Is it true you're going to California this summer?"

"Maybe," replied Marvin, cautiously. "I've got a lot of cousins there." He tried to tiptoe around Hank, but the big bully stuck his foot out, and Marvin tripped right over it.

"Well, have a nice trip!" said Hank, sneering.

Marvin flew forward and crashed into a wall. Hank just stood there and watched. It was obvious that he was pretty impressed with himself.

Scratch and Sniff were impressed, too. "Good one, dude!" they shouted and then congratulated Hank with a high-five.

Marvin peeled himself off the wall. He scowled and growled. "You JERK!"

"I'd rather be a jerk than a klutz, Klutzer!" roared Hank, and he shoved Marvin into

George the janitor's broom closet, kicking the door shut. "See ya next fall!"

Inside the closet, Marvin huffed and puffed. "One of these days I'm going to prove to Hank that I'm not a klutz! Maybe even today!"

CHAPTER TWO
WHAT'S FOR LUNCH

Marvin's favorite time of the day was finally here. Lunchtime. And after a morning full of math problems, Marvin couldn't wait to get in the cafeteria line.

Ulysses was hungry, too. "What are you getting, Marvin? A Cheesey-Chiliburger or a Ham-Slam sandwich?"

"Both," said Marvin.

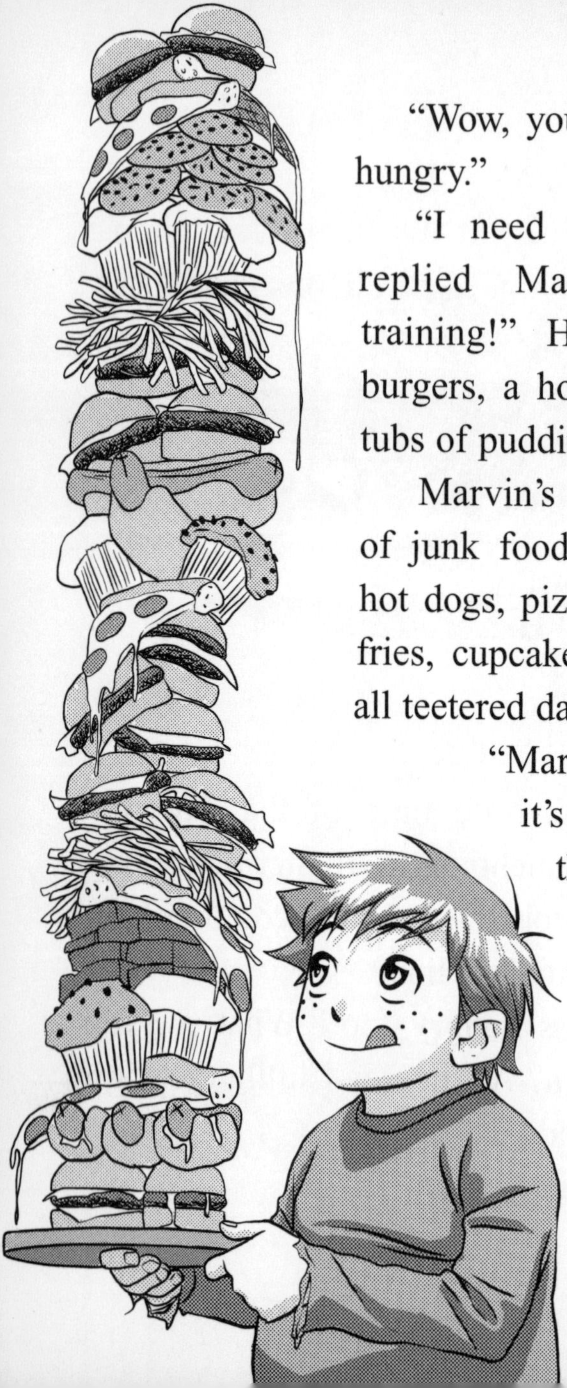

"Wow, you must be super-hungry."

"I need lots of energy," replied Marvin. "I'm in training!" He dumped two burgers, a hot dog, and three tubs of pudding on his tray.

Marvin's tray was a tower of junk food. Cheeseburgers, hot dogs, pizza slices, French fries, cupcakes, and brownies all teetered dangerously.

"Marvin, do you think it's healthy to eat all that stuff?" asked Ulysses.

"It's like what Coach Crunch always says, 'Food is fuel for growing muscles.' And I need lots of muscles. It's all part of my training program."

Ulysses smiled at his hero. "I'm gonna train, too." He plopped two burgers and a hot dog onto his own tray.

Marvin carefully led Ulysses toward their table.

"Wow!" exclaimed a second grader, staring at Marvin's tray. "You gonna eat all that?"

"Yep!" said Marvin, chomping on a burger.

"And what Marvin doesn't finish, I will," Ulysses said. "We're in training!"

"Yo, Klutzer!" called Hank, stomping over to Marvin. "Leave some food for the rest of us!"

"We're gonna call you 'Chubs' instead of Klutz!" laughed Scratch.

"Aw, let him stuff his face," said Sniff. "I wanna see him explode!" He laughed and sneezed at the same time, spraying the table.

The Terrible Trio was howling with laughter as they left the cafeteria.

"Hank is a real pain," grumbled Marvin.

"Don't worry," said Ulysses. "Once you toughen up, Hank will get his just deserts."

"Dessert? Good idea!" Marvin reached for a big fat brownie that stuck out from the bottom of his food pile.

"Aren't you gonna eat the stuff on top first?" asked Ulysses.

"I can't wait!" said Marvin, and he plucked out the brownie.

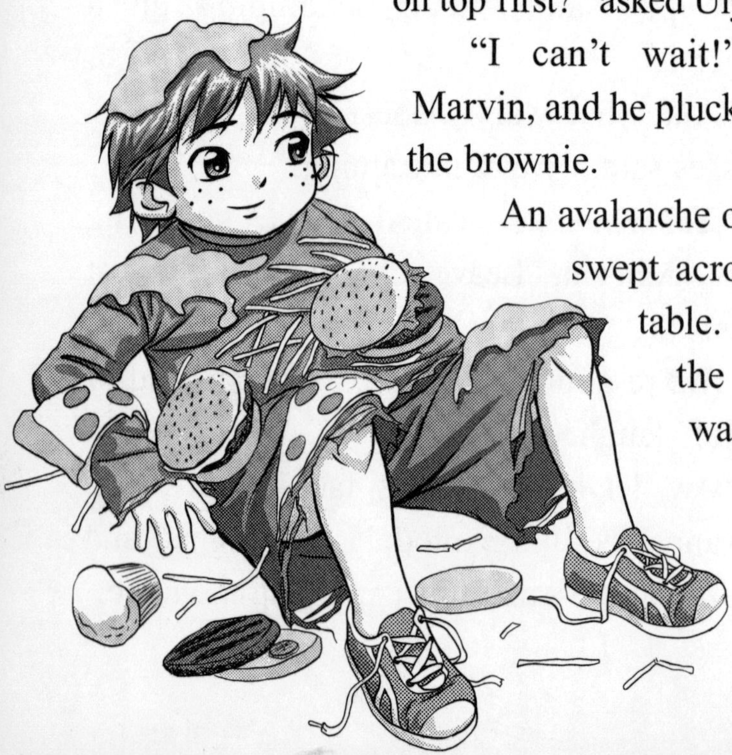

An avalanche of food swept across the table. When the slide was over, everyone next to Marvin was covered with mustard, fries, pizza, and pudding. "Sorry," apologized Marvin.

"That's okay," said Ulysses. "It was an accident. No biggie. I'll help you clean up."

Marvin was pleased. As always, Ulysses was there for him.

The Terrible Trio was there, too. They must've heard the noise, wondered what all the ruckus was about, and decided to come back. "Klutz! Klutz!" they chanted. "Klutzer the Klutz!"

"Those guys will be sorry," Marvin said. "Because I'm not going to be a klutz forever!"

CHAPTER THREE
MARVIN'S BIG IDEA

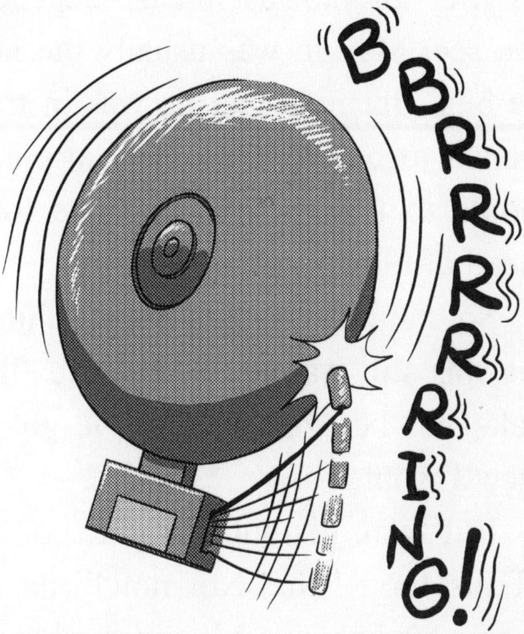
BBRRRRRING!

The final school bell rang and everyone practically flew out of the building.

"Outta my way!" screamed Marvin, at the top of his lungs. He took off so fast that Ulysses couldn't even get a word out before he was already halfway down the block.

Yes. Marvin was running! And he was doing it so quickly that one might even think his life—or his last meal—depended on it. You see, Marvin was usually the last one on the bus. But now that he was in training, he wanted to be the first. He had places to go, people to talk to, and a whole lot of work ahead of him.

So, naturally, it was a good thing that the bus was still waiting at the curb. "I'm gonna make it!" he exclaimed as he got closer. "I knew I would—"

But then, his untied right shoe flew right off his foot. "No! Not now!" he screamed. Losing his balance, Marvin fumbled and went flying to the ground.

Like a stampeding herd of cows, kids charged past Marvin, who was nothing but a big, messy heap in the middle of the crowd.

But by the time Marvin managed to pull himself together and get up off the sidewalk, the bus was long gone.

"Looks like we missed it again," said Ulysses, as he finally joined his pal.

"I wanted to walk anyway," replied Marvin.

"Oh, me, too," said Ulysses.

And so the two walked on, each trying to convince the other that traveling by bus was not nearly as good for training as a brisk walk.

"Plus, now we have time to talk about Hank and the others," Marvin said. "I wonder who smells the worst?"

"Definitely Scratch," said Ulysses.

"You think? I'd say Sniff comes in a close second," added Marvin.

"And what about—"

Just then, a familiar voice called out from around the corner. "Yo, dorks!"

It was Hank. But he wasn't after Marvin and Ulysses. The Terrible Trio had surrounded Bobby and Robby, a couple of second-graders.

"No one gets past me without kissing my shoe," Hank threatened.

Marvin and Ulysses hid behind a school dumpster and watched the bully in action. "Why's Hank so nasty?" wondered Ulysses.

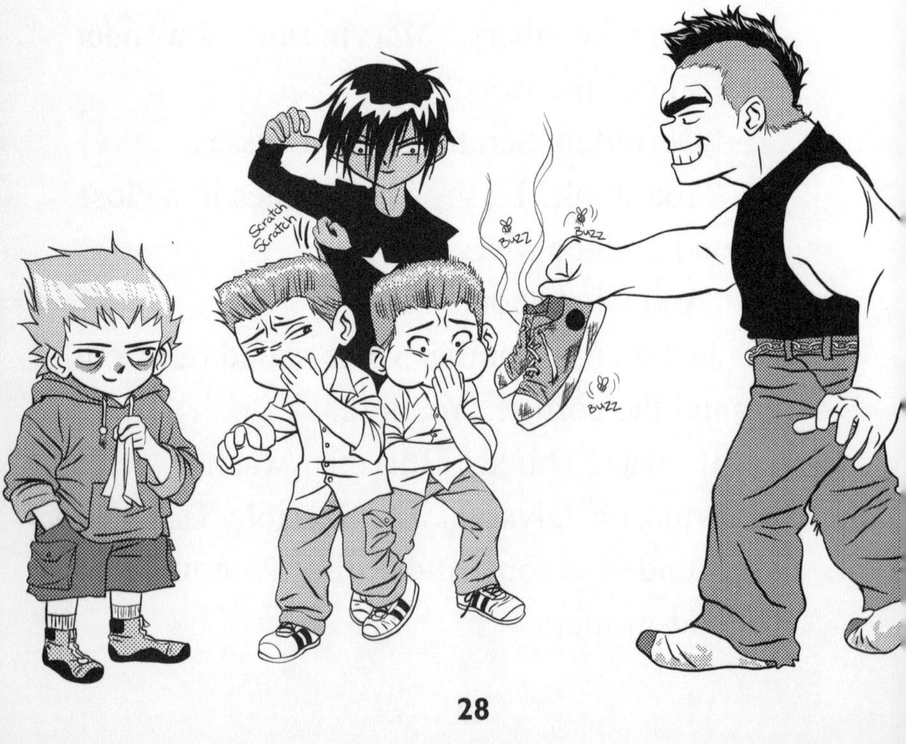
Scratch
Scratch
Buzz
Buzz
Buzz

"His older brother bullies him around all the time," said Marvin. "So, I figure, it's a family thing."

"That still doesn't give him the right to push us around," said Ulysses. "Someone should stop him."

"And that someone should be me!" declared Marvin. "I have just the plan . . ."

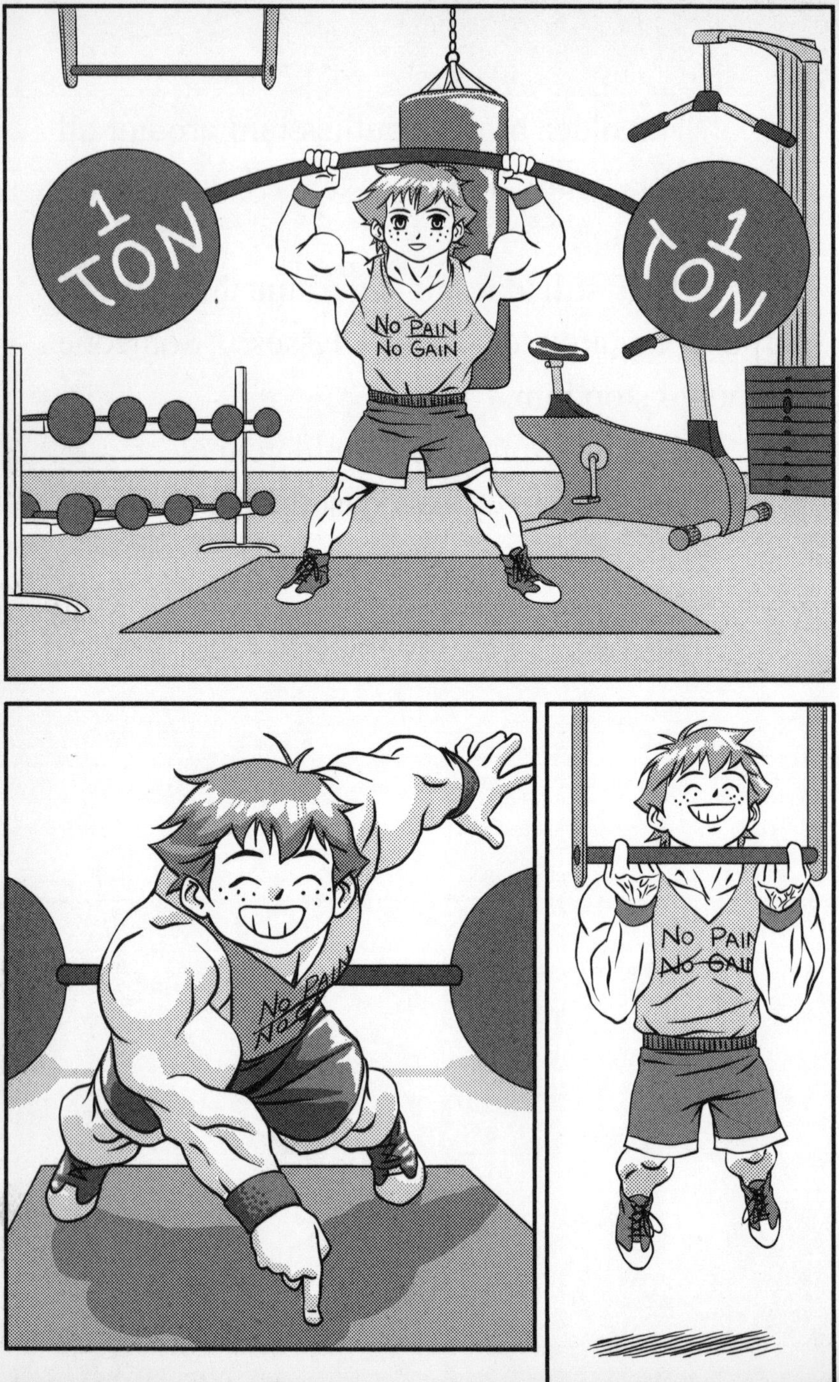
1 TON
1 TON
NO PAIN
NO GAIN

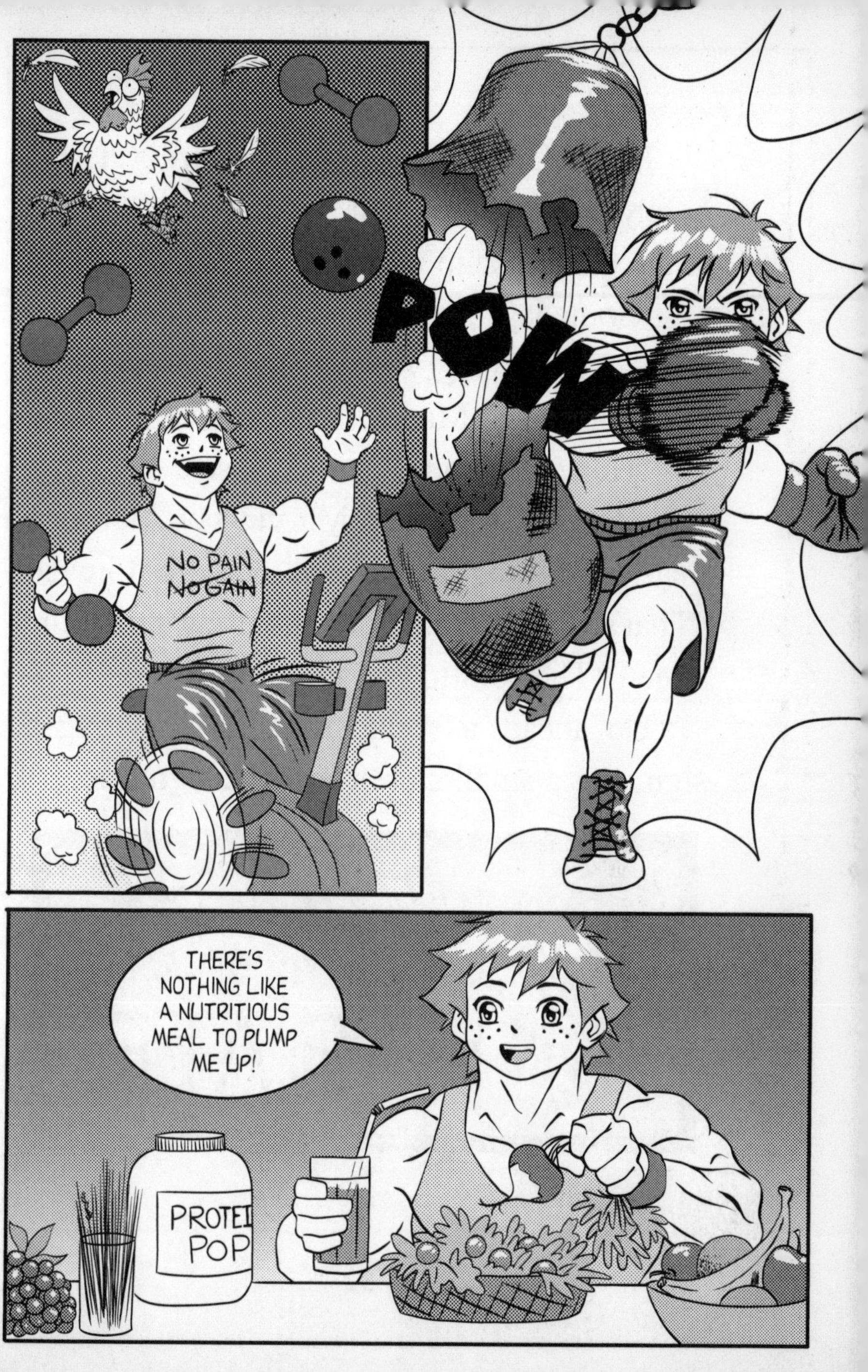
NO PAIN
NO GAIN
POW
THERE'S NOTHING LIKE A NUTRITIOUS MEAL TO PUMP ME UP!
PROTEI
POP

But, Marvin wasn't quite there yet. He barely even knew what vegetables were, let alone that a turnip might be one.

"Someday I'm gonna make that creep sorry for bullying you and me and everyone else," promised Marvin.

"Hopefully soon," said Ulysses.

And that was when Marvin saw the thing that was going to change his life forever. "That's it!" he exclaimed, pointing down the street. "The solution to all our problems!"

Up ahead, a young man was hoisting a sign over a small storefront. The sign said:

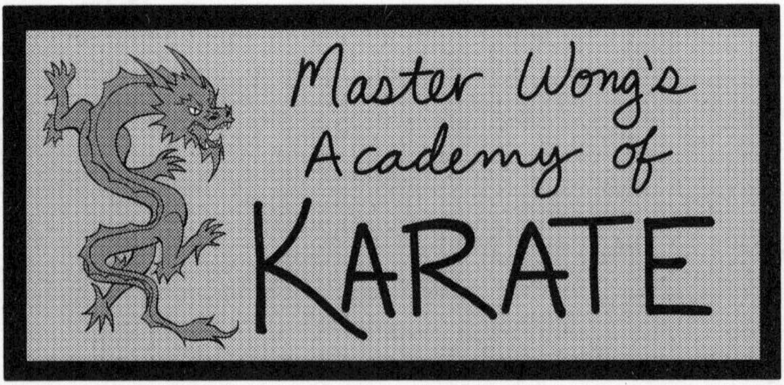
Master Wong's
Academy of
KARATE

"I'm gonna learn karate," announced Marvin. "And then no one will ever mess with me. NO ONE!"

"I want to join, too!" cheered Ulysses.

"Excellent," said Marvin, high-fiving his pal. "All we need is permission from our parents."

Excited, Marvin jumped into the air. He was actually good at jumping . . . it was his landings that needed work. With a thud he slammed down on his butt.

"You okay, Marvin?"

"I'm cool," he said, springing to his feet. "I'm *karate* cool!"

As they headed home, Marvin looked back at Master Wong's sign one more time and he smiled. The Hank problem was about to become history.

CHAPTER FOUR

Dinner at the Klutzers

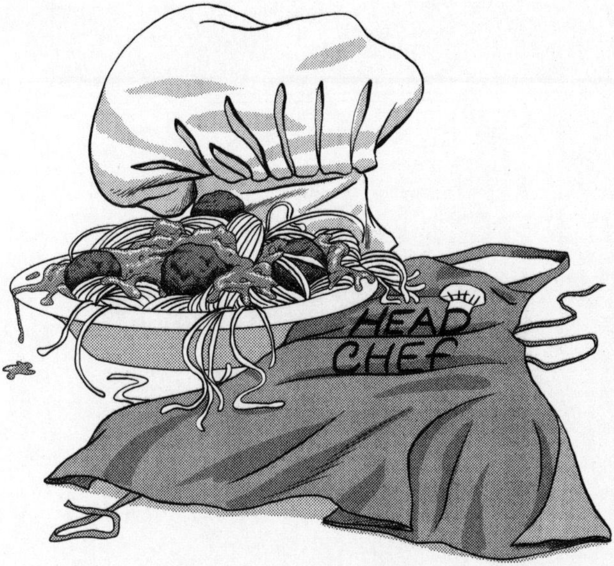
HEAD
CHEF

Marvin loved to eat. There were a lot of things that Marvin wasn't good at, but eating wasn't one of them. From meatballs to sushi, Marvin never met a type of food he didn't like. He especially liked the meals his mom made. As soon as he walked into his house, he could smell dinner. *Fooooood!* he thought, dreamily . . .

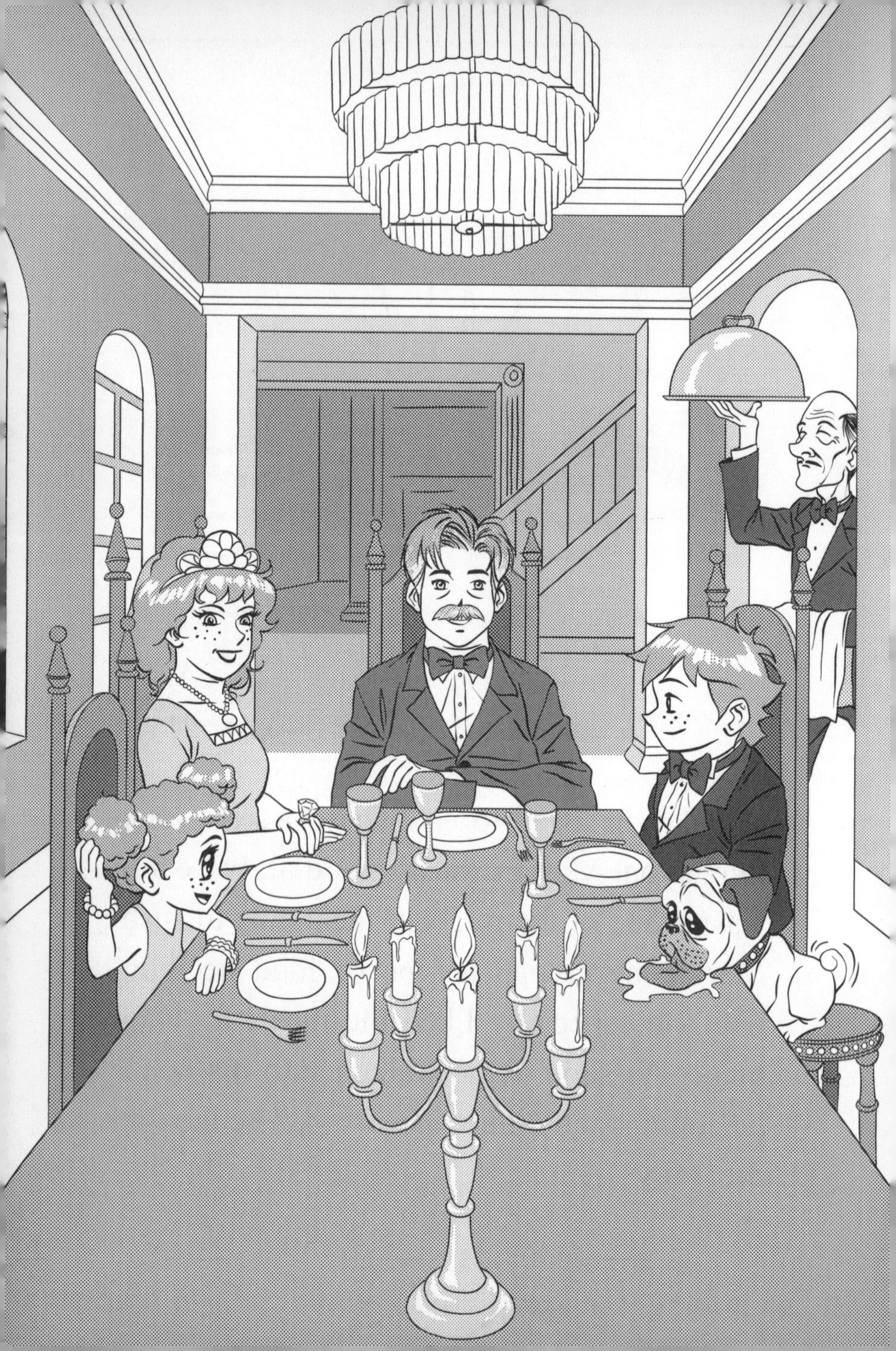

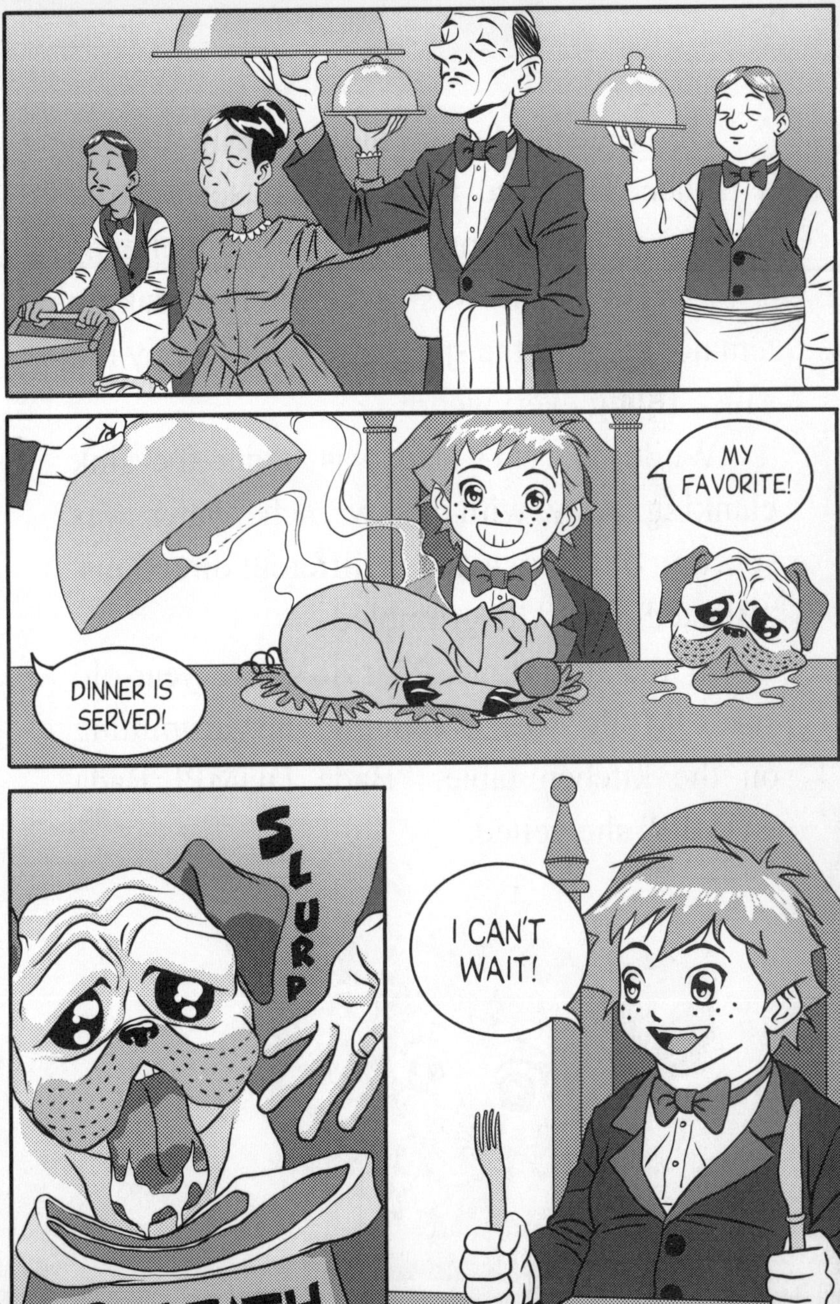
DINNER IS SERVED!
MY FAVORITE!
SLURP
GOLIATH
I CAN'T WAIT!

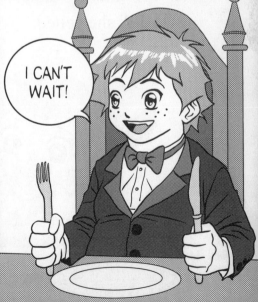

Of course, Marvin didn't really live in a palace. He lived in a tiny house, without butlers, silver serving dishes, or chandeliers.

Marvin's mom was in the kitchen making a major mess of the spaghetti, with gloppy red sauce flying everywhere.

While Marvin's dad was under the sink clanking away with his wrench, water was spurting out from a dozen different directions. "Blasted pipe!" he grumbled.

In the meantime, Marvin's five-year-old sister Molly was practicing her drumming on the kitchen table. "Bada DUMP! Bada BUMP!" she yelled.

“Molly!” shouted Marvin’s mom. “Stop that racket!”

“But percussion is extremely important,” replied Molly, pronouncing each word perfectly. “Without a solid backbeat, music inevitably falls apart. And if I don’t practice my paradiddles, I’ll never be a professional jazz drummer.”

And then, in the middle of all the commotion, was Goliath, the family dog. He was always hungry, always getting into mischief, and always trying to express his innermost-doggie feelings (even if those around him didn’t understand exactly what he was trying to say).

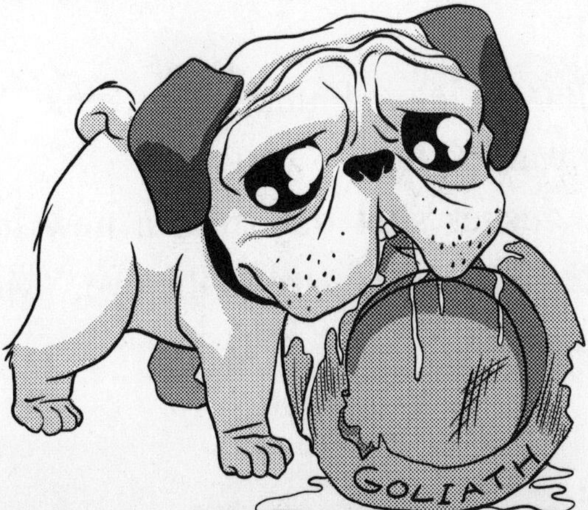
GOLIATH

"Bow-wow!" woofed Goliath, circling his doggie dish.

Marvin was busy taste-testing the meatballs and didn't notice that Goliath was in desperate need of conducting his very own taste test. Finally, he tossed a misshapen meatball into the pug's drooling mouth.

"ARF!" Goliath barked, which means "Deee-lish!" in dog-speak.

Marvin thought it was deee-lish, too, but surprisingly, he had more than food on his mind . . .

"Mom, I want to talk to you about—"

"Can't talk!" she gasped, slamming a lid on a sputtering pot. "Dinner's about to erupt!"

Marvin leaned under the sink. "Dad, I really want to talk to you—"

A gusher shot out from a new leak and squirted Marvin square in the eye. "Mumph!" he mumbled.

"Anything!"

"Sign me up for karate class."

"Deal!"

Marvin was thrilled. He was on his way to becoming a world-class bully-butt-kicking karate expert. His days of playing the role of "klutz" were numbered!

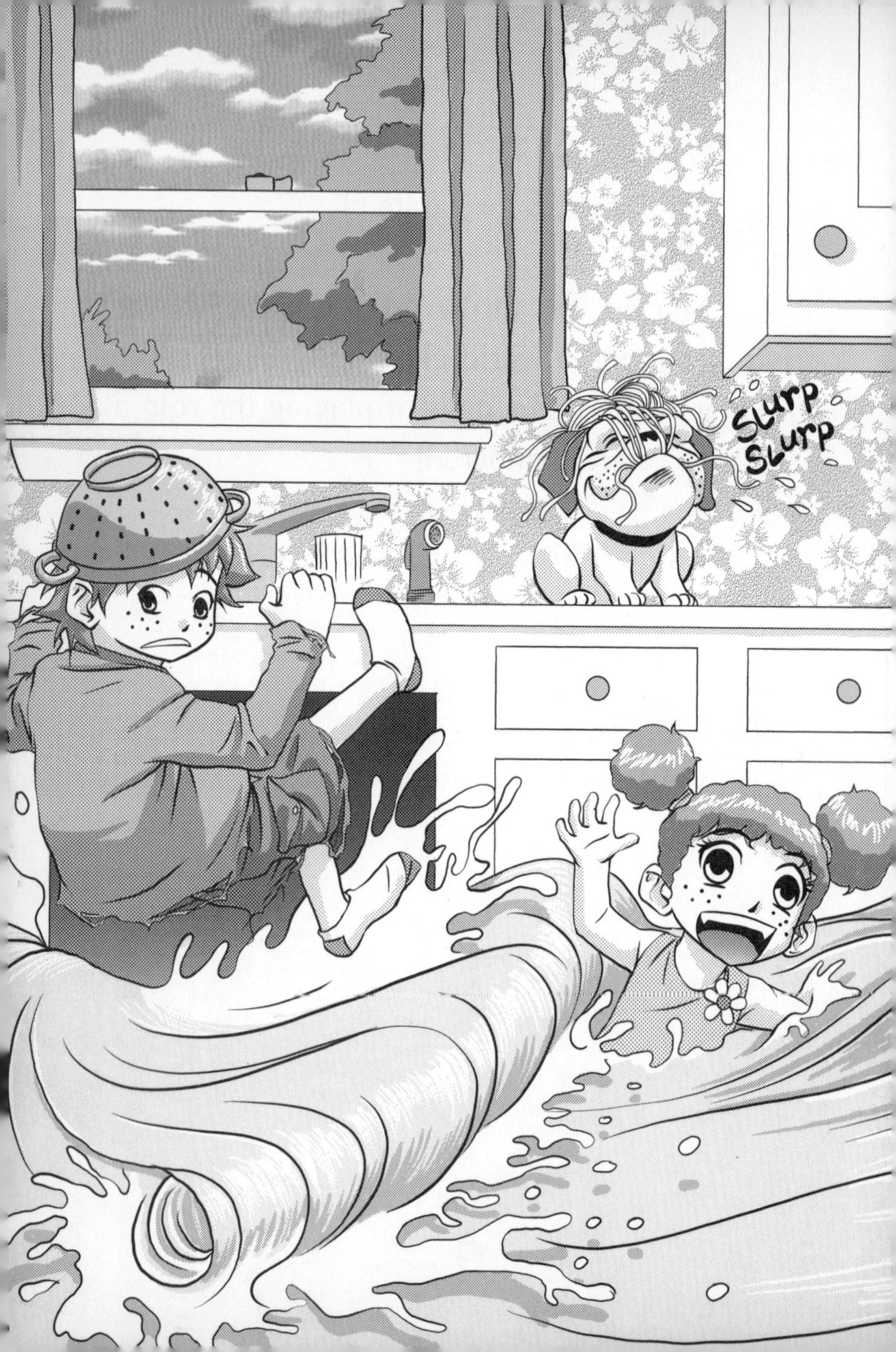
SLURP
SLURP

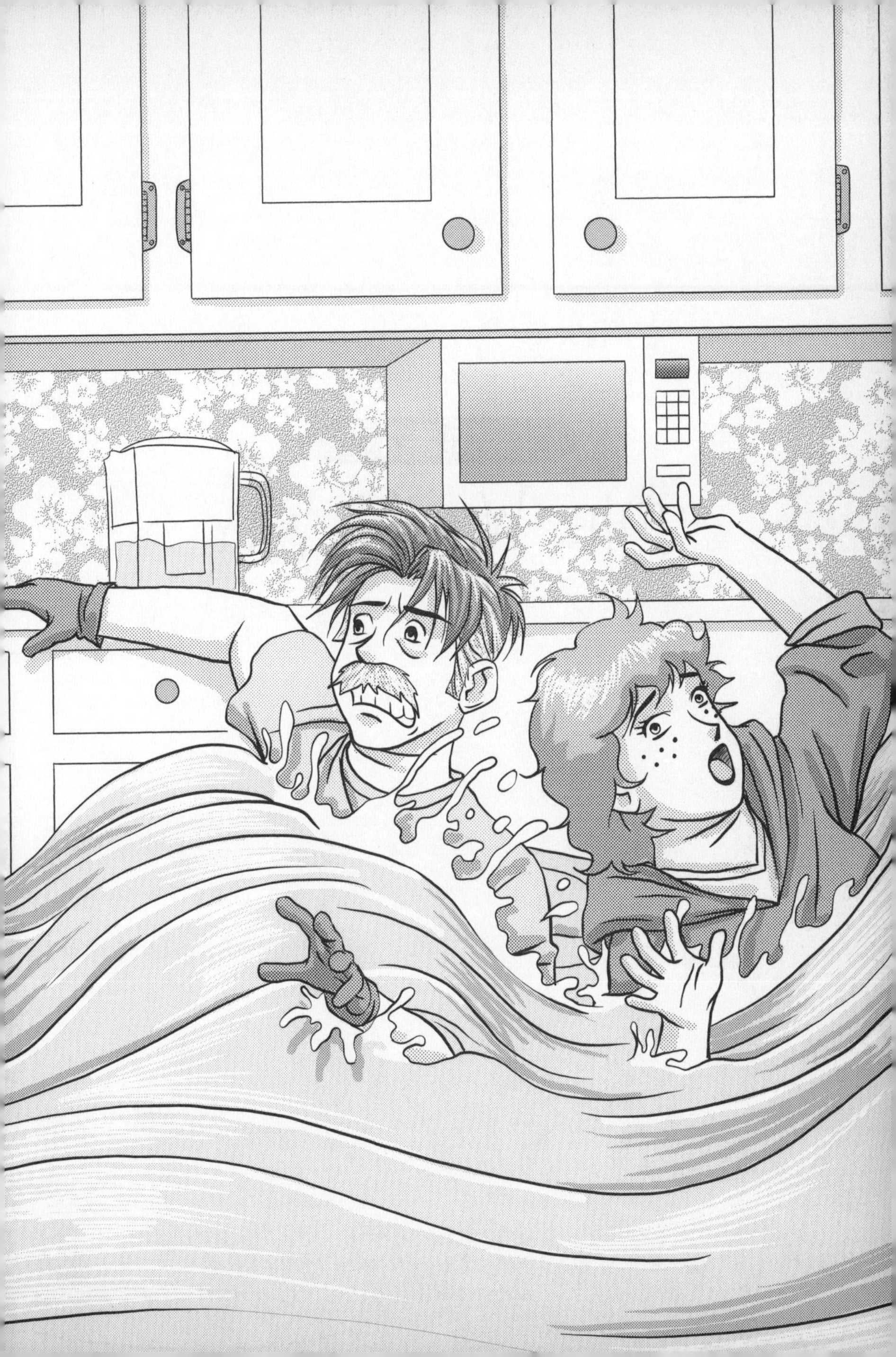

CHAPTER FIVE

THE WONG WAY

"Hai-YAH!" Marvin burst into Master Wong's Academy of Karate. He was super-excited. Inside this *dojo*, (which is the Japanese word for the space where you practice martial arts) he was going to learn all the ancient secrets of karate.

"Over here, Marvin!" waved Ulysses. He was sitting in the front of the class and saving his pal a spot.

"Marvin," whispered Ulysses. "Your *obi!* It's not tied!"

"Obi?!" said Marvin. "What's an obi?" And then he remembered that it's the Japanese word for *belt*. Ulysses was right, Marvin's obi was flopping off his pants. As he twirled

around to pick up the end, he toppled over and rolled across the floor.

Marvin's tumble was stopped by a wall. Only this wall wasn't made out of bricks or stones. It was soft, fleshy, and had a bad temper. It was Master Wong himself.

"Marvin Klutzer, here! Ready to rumble!"

Master Wong smiled. "Not so fast, Marvin," he said, patiently. He turned to the class.

"I am Master Wong, your *sensei,* or teacher. Before we begin class, we must first bow to each other. It is both a greeting and a sign of respect."

Master Wong then demonstrated by bowing to the room of students.

"Got it!" exclaimed Marvin, and he jerked his head down. Unfortunately, his bow was way too fast, and he bonked his noggin against Master Wong's.

"OUCH!"

"Sorry," said Marvin, as Master Wong massaged his forehead. "So what's next? Elbow smashes? Roundhouse punches? What about breaking bricks with one finger and smashing the bad guys?"

"Karate isn't about breaking bricks or heads," said Master Wong. "*Karate* means *empty hand*. That's what we use to defend ourselves."

But Marvin wasn't listening. He was too busy hopping around the room like a kangaroo on a trampoline and jabbing imaginary opponents with his fists . . .

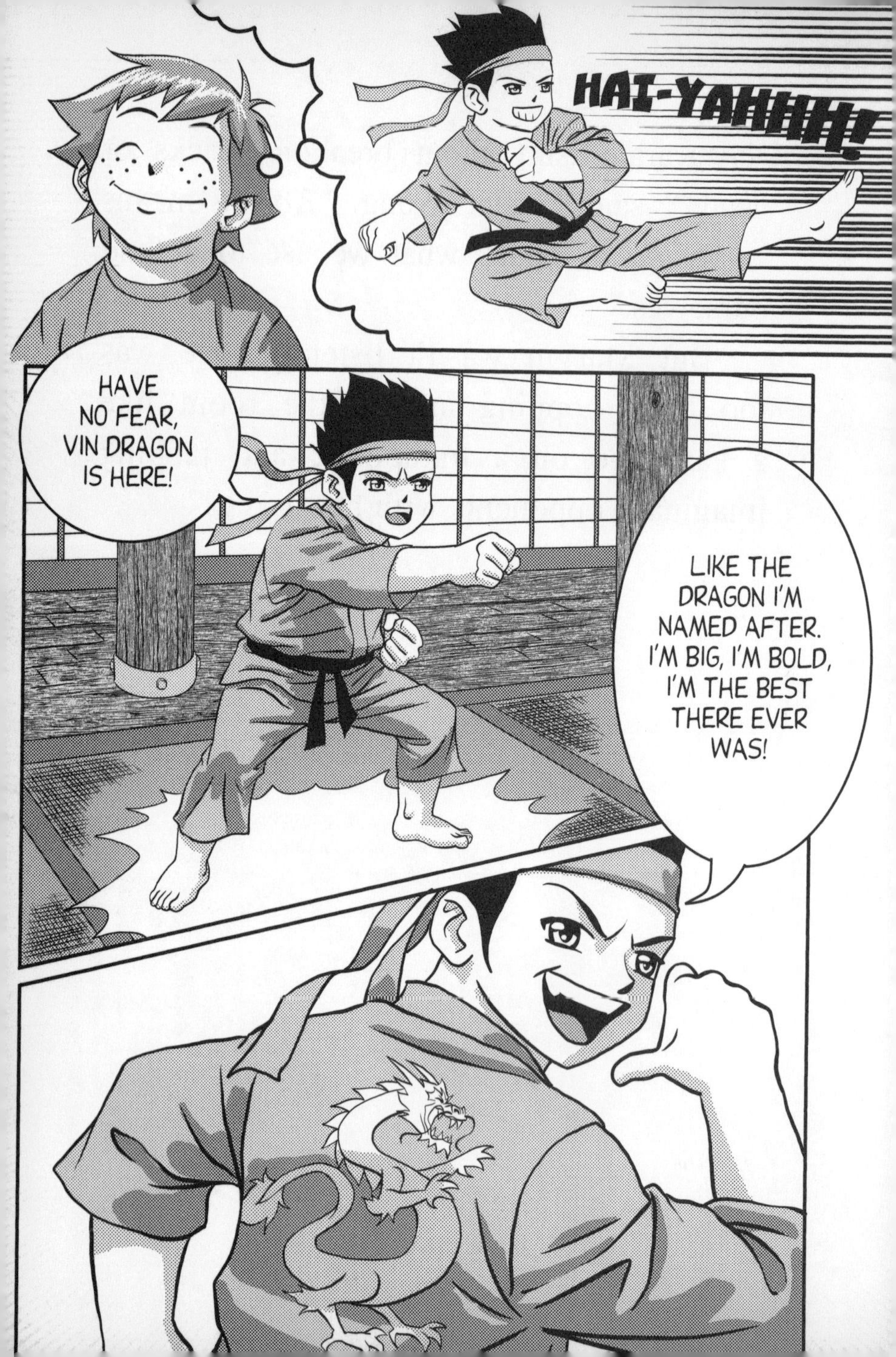
HAI-YAHHHH!
HAVE NO FEAR, VIN DRAGON IS HERE!
LIKE THE DRAGON I'M NAMED AFTER. I'M BIG, I'M BOLD, I'M THE BEST THERE EVER WAS!

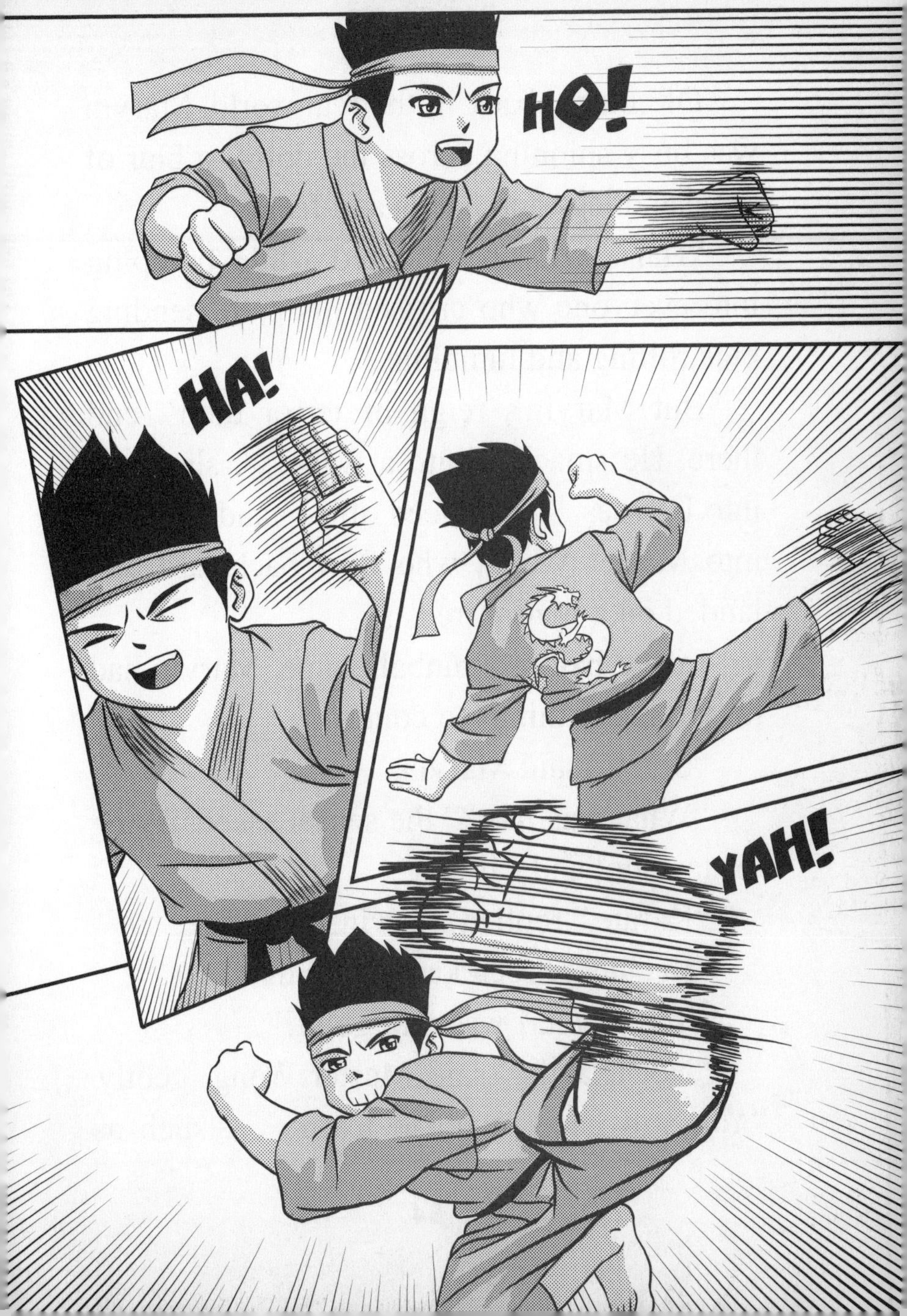
HO!
HA!
YAH!

Of course, back in the real world, Marvin was busy spinning across the dojo—a blur of arms and legs and hands and feet.

"Hai-YAH!" he shouted while bumping into everyone who crossed his path, sending kids rolling and tumbling.

But Marvin's reign of terror didn't end there. He smacked into a wall . . . slammed into Ulysses . . . bounced off . . . and rammed into Master Wong, who flew backward and landed on a bonsai tree.

Like a ball in a pinball game, Marvin had hit too many things to count.

"Sorry," said Marvin.

"What was *that?*" the sensei asked, trying to stay cool and calm.

"Karate," replied Marvin.

"I've never seen karate like that."

"You mean, I was *that* good?"

"Not exactly," said Master Wong, gently. "You still have much to learn . . . such as patience. See you all tomorrow," he groaned as he stood up.

Marvin was feeling disappointed. "Too bad we couldn't keep going. I was just getting warmed up." Marvin said as he watched everyone leave the dojo.

"Me, too," said Ulysses, flexing his fingers.

Marvin puffed up his chest. "Just stick with me and do what I do, Ulysses," he said. "And you'll become a karate expert, too!"

CHAPTER SIX

Kung Fu, Anyone?

The next day, the school bus pulled up to the curb and, as usual, everyone piled out in one big rush. Of course, Marvin was the last one to get off. But something was different about him.

Ulysses was the first to notice. "You didn't tumble. You didn't trip. Your pants aren't even falling down!"

"My klutzy days are over," said Marvin. "Just call me, karate cool."

"Wow," said Ulysses. "And you've only had one lesson."

"I'm a fast learner," bragged Marvin. "Karate comes naturally to me."

Ulysses nodded. The future seemed bright for his hero and friend . . . at least it did until they got to gym class.

"Look alive, ladies!" roared Coach Crunch.

Today, the cranky coach had a special event planned: a volleyball game between the third and fourth graders. That meant Marvin's team was going up against Hank's.

"Hank doesn't look happy," Ulysses whispered to his pal.

"Hank *never* looks happy," replied Marvin. "I almost feel sorry for him."

"Klutzer!" called out Hank. "What are *you* doing here? This is the gym, not the cafeteria!"

Marvin frowned. "Forget what I said about feeling sorry, Ulysses."

TWEEEET! Coach Crunch blew his whistle. The game was on!

The volleyball shot back and forth over the net, whizzing through the air. Everyone was having fun. That is, until Hank got control of the ball.

"Heads up, Klutz!" he yelled, hurling the ball at Marvin. Hank had excellent aim.

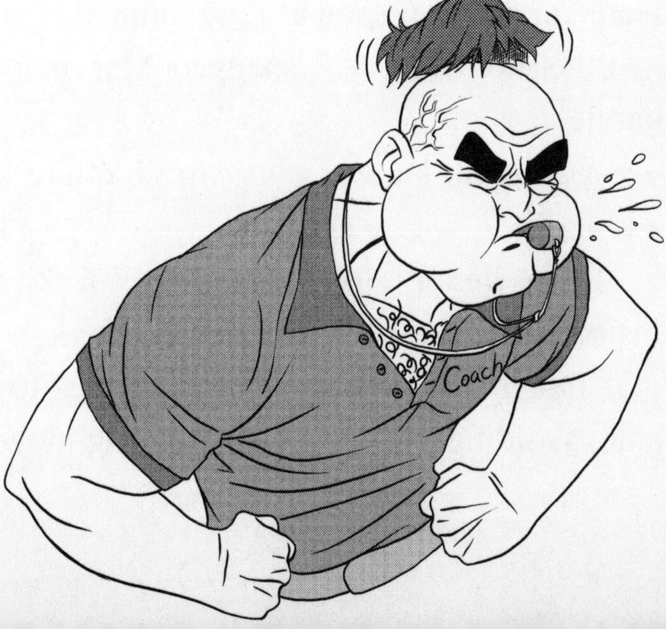
Coach

After getting hit about a gazillion times, Marvin yelled, "Time out!"

"Need to change your diaper, Klutz?" teased Hank.

"No!" said Marvin. "But *you're* gonna need to change *yours* in a minute."

And without thinking about what he was doing, Marvin lunged at Hank.

Marvin was crazily spinning around the court, his arms and feet jabbing the air. "Hai-YAH!"

"Check out Kung Fu Klutz!" shouted Hank, as Marvin spun around him.

"It's not kung fu," snapped Marvin. "It's karate!"

"Kung fu, karate, who cares? You're still a klutz!"

"You better stop calling me a klutz," insisted Marvin, swinging toward Hank.

"Oooh, I'm shaking!" Hank dodged to the side, avoiding Marvin's wild twirling moves.

"GAME OVER!!!" bellowed Coach Crunch, blowing his whistle. TWEEEET!

"Klutzer!" roared Coach Crunch. "You're supposed to be playing volleyball, not practicing kung fu!"

"It's not kung fu," corrected Marvin, still hopping up and down. "It's karate."

"Okay, Mr. Expert, you want to show off your mad skills? You can demonstrate them for the entire school on Friday," threatened Coach Crunch. "CLASS DISMISSED!" he barked.

"Maybe Hank is right," sighed Marvin. "I'm just a Kung Fu Klutz."

"No way," countered Ulysses. "You're still karate cool to me."

"No," muttered Marvin. "I'm the Klutzer that totally klutzed out!"

For once, Ulysses didn't know what to say to make his friend feel better.

CHAPTER SEVEN
BUTTERFLY FLIGHT

Marvin burst into Master Wong's dojo and
marched right up to the sensei.

"Karate's not working for me! I punched,
I blocked, but I still got smacked down! And I
need to be a karate master by Friday!"

"You need to be patient," he said. "It takes
time for the caterpillar to turn into a butterfly."

A butterfly? thought Marvin. *Hmmm . . .*

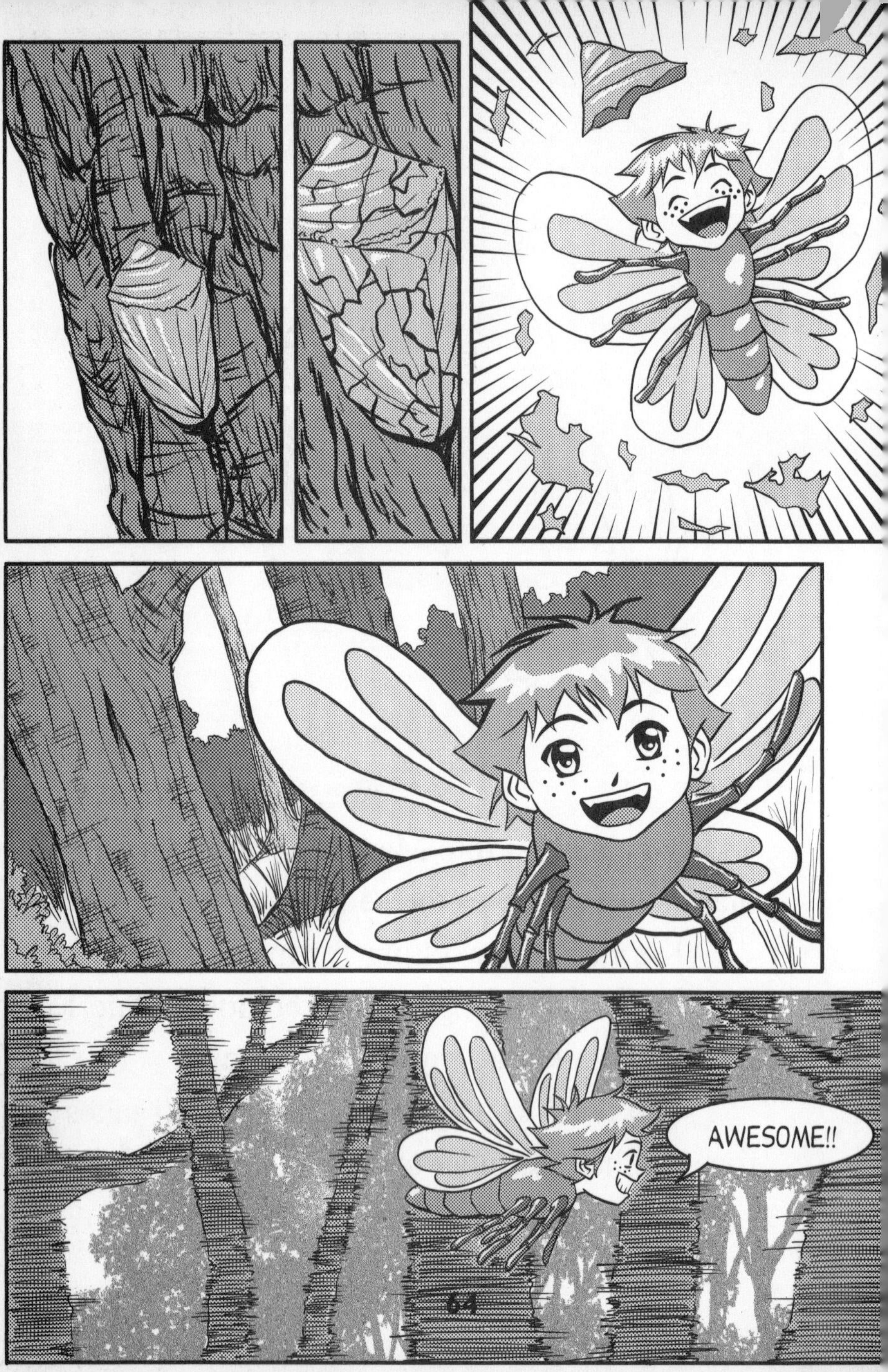
AWESOME!!

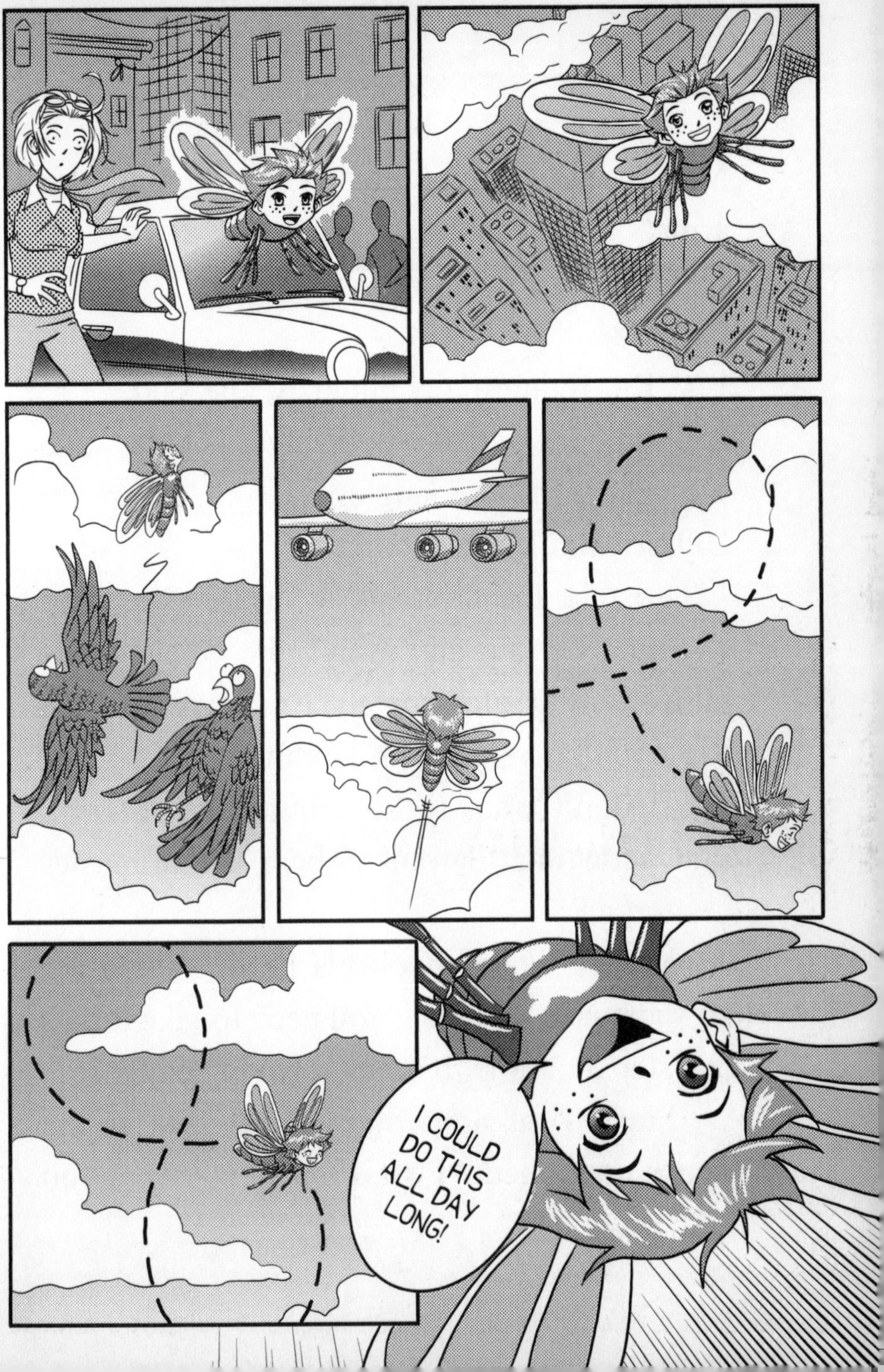
I COULD DO THIS ALL DAY LONG!

With visions of butterflies still in his head, Marvin ran around the room, flapping his arms. "Wheeeee!"

"Marvin, what're you doing?!" called Ulysses.

"I'm flying like a butterfly," he said.

Someone yelled out "Klutzer is nuts!" and soon everyone was laughing at him, except for Ulysses and Master Wong.

Lost in his thoughts, Marvin leapt onto a stool. "Up, up and away!" he yelled as he jumped off. Unfortunately, it was a very short flight with a very rough landing.

"I don't want to be a butterfly," Marvin said, scowling. "I want to be a karate master . . . *today*!"

Master Wong shook his head. "There are no short-cuts in karate. You need to take things one step at a time. It's called having patience."

Marvin sat down next to Ulysses as the sensei continued. "First, *think* about what you want to do before you do it. Then, once you have a plan, you can move forward. Think like the *caterpillar*, not the butterfly."

So, like a caterpillar, Marvin took things one step at a time. However, his steps were way different than anyone else's.

When Marvin kicked, he wasn't patient enough to think about where he was and he accidentally stepped on Master Wong's toe.

When Marvin spun, he wasn't patient enough to think about where he was going and he slammed into a shelf of teacups. In a mad flurry, they went crashing to the floor.

And when Marvin rolled backward, he wasn't patient enough to double-check his belt. In fact, he had forgotten to wear it!

His pants slid down, and he quickly got tangled up in his gi. Like a bowling ball, he knocked over kids, one by one.

"Guess I need a little more work on that caterpillar thing," admitted Marvin.

"A little?" sighed Master Wong, rolling his eyes. "I'd say a lot!" He handed a broom and dustpan to Marvin. "For your first lesson in patience, help me clean up this mess!"

Marvin started sweeping. But instead of thinking about patience, he thought about what he was going to do to Hank. *He's going down!* Marvin smiled smugly.

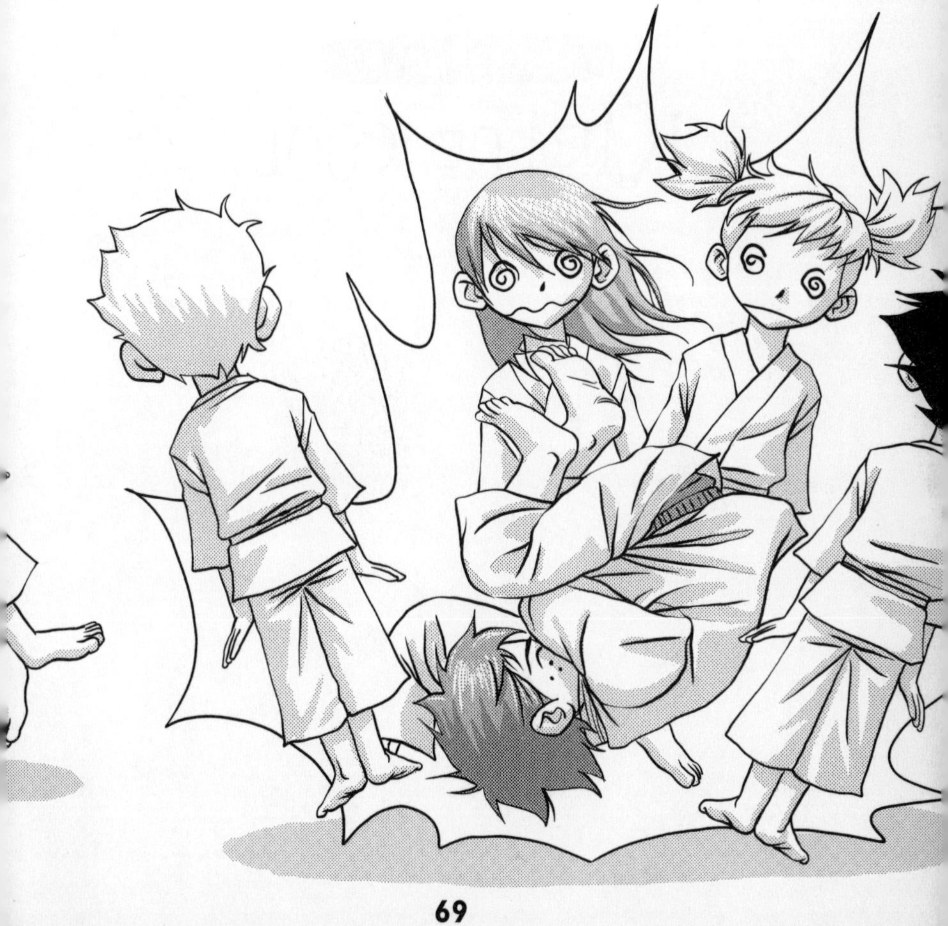

CHAPTER EIGHT

KARATE COOL

The school gym was packed with kids. "Klutzer's Karate Friday" was here!

"Three cheers for Marvin!" shouted Molly, sitting courtside. "Hip-hip-hooray!"

Hank, Scratch, and Sniff were stomping their feet. "We want Kung Fu Klutz!" they chanted. Soon, the whole place was yelling, "We want Kung Fu Klutz!"

Coach Crunch blasted his whistle. TWEEEET! "It's time, people!"

Molly whipped out her drumsticks and banged out a fast drumroll.

Like sports stars, Marvin and Ulysses made their grand entrance. They walked onto the court waving to the crowd.

"Bring it on, Kung Fu Klutz!" hollered Hank.

"It's not kung fu, it's karate!" Marvin yelled back. He turned to face Ulysses, and they bowed to each other. "*Hajime!*" Marvin shouted. That means, "Let's begin!"

The boys began to spar. A hush spread over the crowd as Marvin and Ulysses traded punches, kicks, and blocking moves. It almost looked like they were dancing. The amazing thing was that Marvin wasn't klutzy at all.

"Go, Marvin, GO!" cheered Molly.

But the Terrible Trio was not impressed. "Show-off!" they heckled in unison.

Smirking, Hank pulled out a bag of gumballs. "Watch this, guys," he said, flinging a handful onto the floor. "Operation Klutz-Out is a go!"

Marvin, who was on the court spinning and kicking, slid on some of the gumballs.

He lurched forward and into Ulysses, who fell and skidded backward across the gym. When Ulysses stopped, his pants were around his ankles. "Uh oh!" he squealed.

The crowd roared with laughter. The Terrible Trio stood up and shouted at the top of their lungs, "We see London, we see France, we see Ulysses' underpants!"

Totally embarrassed, Ulysses ran out of the gym.

"Sorry, Klutzer," said Coach Crunch. "Looks like your little demo is over."

"No it's not," said Scratch, running up.

"We got a replacement for Ulysses," sniffled Sniff.

Marvin whirled around. "NO WAY!"

"Yes, way," said Hank, who was now wearing a gi similar to Marvin's. "You're not the only one who knows kung fu, Klutz."

"It's not kung fu, it's *karate!*" hollered Marvin. And he leapt at Hank. "Hai!"

Marvin whirled around like a top. "You're going down!"

"Ya think?" said Hank. With a lightning-fast move, he kicked his foot out, sweeping under Marvin's legs. "You're the one who's going down, Kung Fu Klutz!"

For a second, Marvin caught air—his feet were off the ground. Then he crashed, hitting the floor like a ton of bricks.

Dazed, Marvin shook his head. He could hear voices, like his sister Molly who was yelling, "Marvin! Get up!" Most of the other voices, however, were yelling "Kung Fu Klutz! Kung Fu Klutz!"

But one voice was louder than the rest. It was Master Wong's. "Remember . . . patience. One step at a time. Think like the caterpillar, not the butterfly."

Marvin began to think really hard. He closed his eyes and tried to concentrate. *Caterpillar . . . caterpillar . . .*

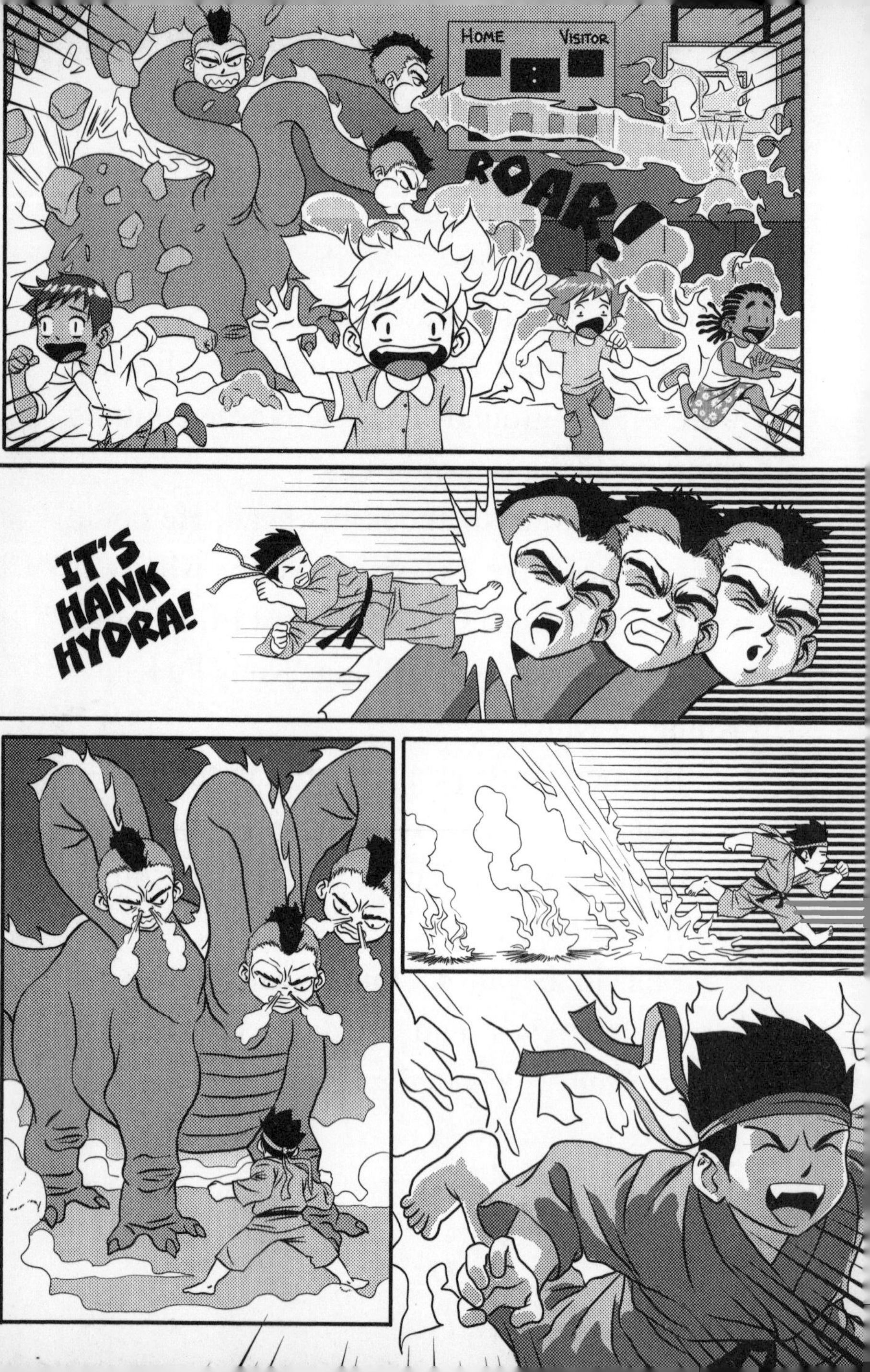
HOME
VISITOR
ROAR!
IT'S HANK HYDRA!

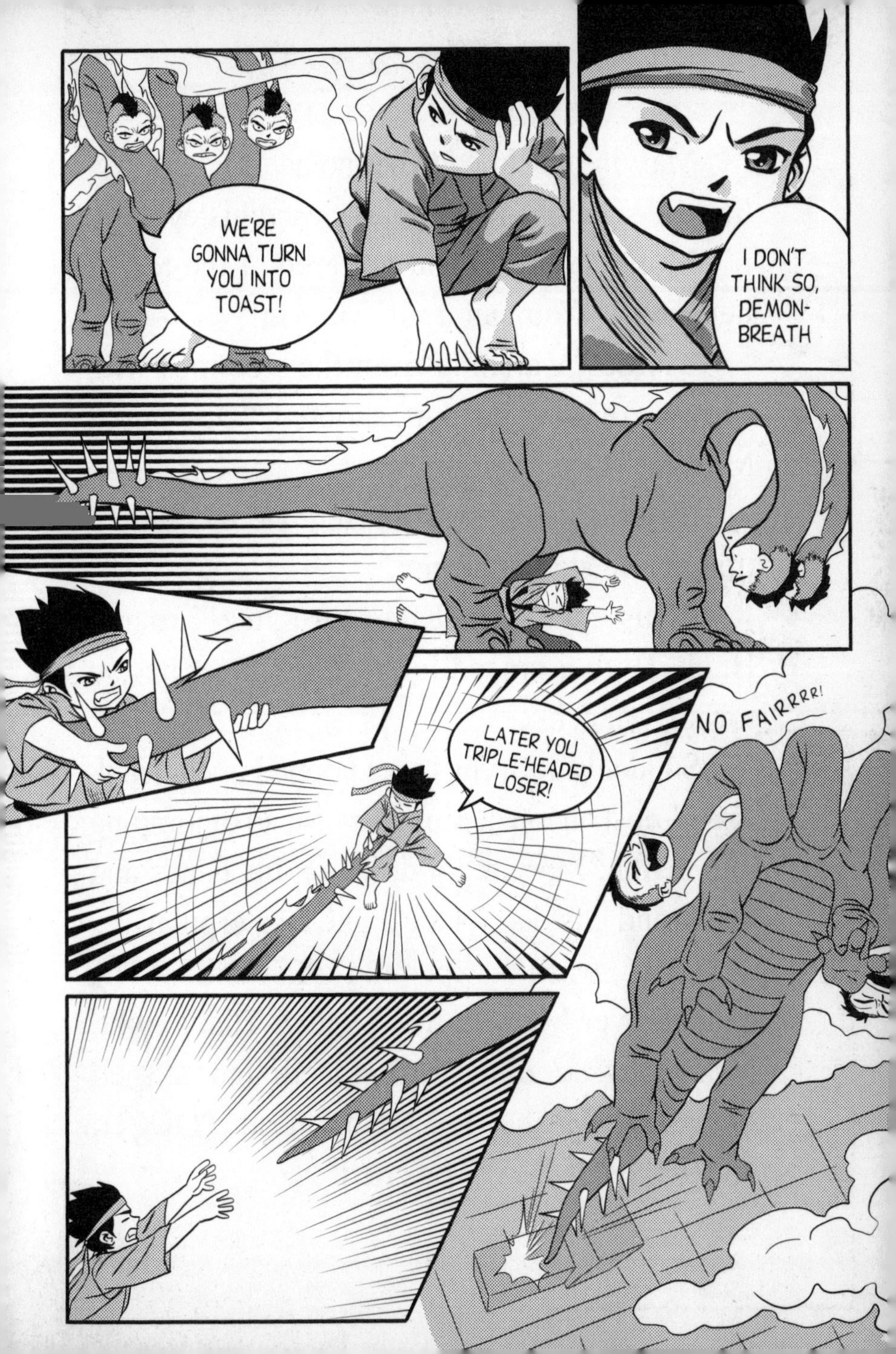
WE'RE GONNA TURN YOU INTO TOAST!
I DON'T THINK SO, DEMON-BREATH
LATER YOU TRIPLE-HEADED LOSER!
NO FAIRRRR!

Marvin now knew what he had to do in real life. He sat cross-legged and closed his eyes.

Molly stood up and hollered at the top of her lungs, "You can do it, Marvin!"

Ulysses, watching from the sidelines with a towel covering his butt, shouted, "Don't quit, Marvin!"

But Marvin wasn't quitting. He was taking things one step at a time.

"This ends here, Kung Fu Klutz!" roared Hank. With a crazed look on his face, he ran toward Marvin.

Suddenly, Marvin's eyes popped open. Hank was almost on top of him. But instead of jumping into action, Marvin got down on his hands and knees and crawled forward like a caterpillar.

Hank wasn't expecting this and so he tripped over Marvin, like a klutz. That's right, *Hank klutzed out!* He bumped into a shelf of basketballs that fell on his head. "OUCH! OOOH! MOMMY!" he cried.

The crowd went wild. "Go Klutzer!" they cheered. "Marvin is marvelous! Klutzer rules!"

Molly was beaming proudly.

Even Coach Crunch was cheering. "Your style is, uh, kind of weird," he said, patting Marvin on the back. "But it works, and that's okay in my book!"

"Hank klutzed out worse than Klutzer ever did!" said Scratch as he scratched his head.

"I hope he's not gonna cry like he did when his brother sat on him," added Sniff. He started to laugh, but then he sneezed all over himself instead. "ACHOO!"

Feeling triumphant, Marvin and Ulysses swaggered over to Hank who was sprawled on the ground.

"Guess I'm not a Kung Fu Klutz anymore," said Marvin, proudly. "I'm Karate Cool!"

"Correction, Marvin," chimed in Ulysses. "You're the Karate COOLEST!"

And all Hank could do was groan.

CHAPTER NINE

MASTER WONG IS NEVER WRONG

Marvin was in a great mood for the rest of the day. As soon as school was over, he ran as fast as he could to the dojo.

Master Wong was surprised to see him, especially since it wasn't even close to the time when karate class started.

"I just wanted to say thanks," said Marvin, bowing. "You were right. I took things one step at a time. I became the caterpillar and I kicked Hank's butt!"

Master Wong laughed. "I'm not so sure about the 'kicking-butt' part, but I'm glad to see you're learning something."

Marvin walked over to the mirror and checked himself out. Vin Dragon was staring back at him. Since Marvin could barely contain his excitement, he did the one thing that seemed to make perfect sense to him—he roared.

"Rrrrr . . . aaarrrrggghhh—"

"—Marvin, your journey has only just begun," continued the sensei. "You might be a caterpillar now, but if you use the Wong Way, you'll eventually turn into a butterfly."

"That's okay, I guess," replied Marvin. "But I'd rather be a dragon. Ferocious, fierce, and furious!"

"Patience, Marvin," reminded Master Wong. "Patience!"

Unfortunately, Marvin hadn't tied his shoelaces . . . again.

The "caterpillar" rolled past Master Wong and crashed into a chair.

"I may be a Klutzer and a klutz," said Marvin. "But I'm still Karate Cool!"

Master Wong nodded. "Karate Cool, indeed!"

BONUS MANGA

GOLIATH THE WONDER DOG?

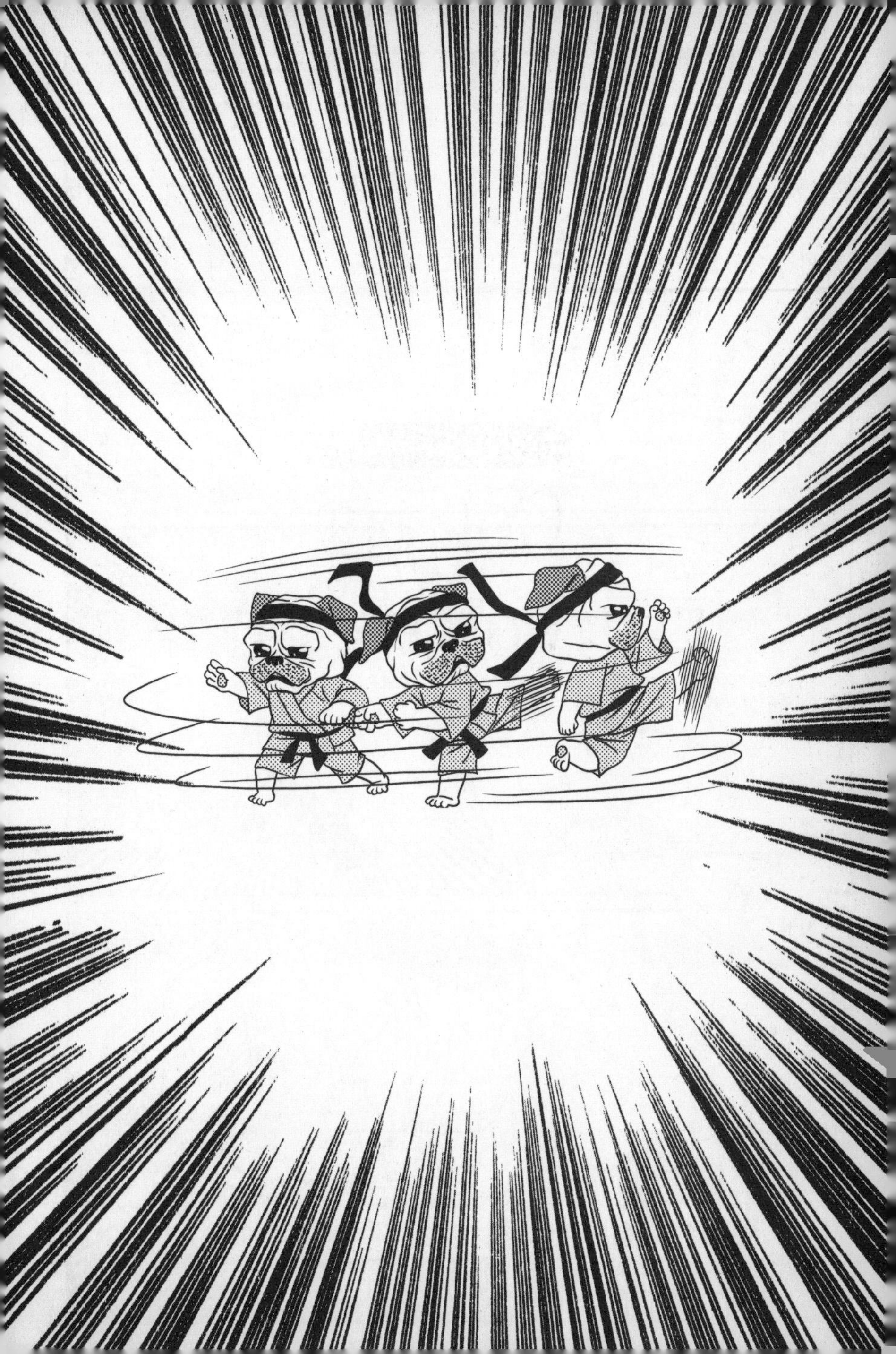

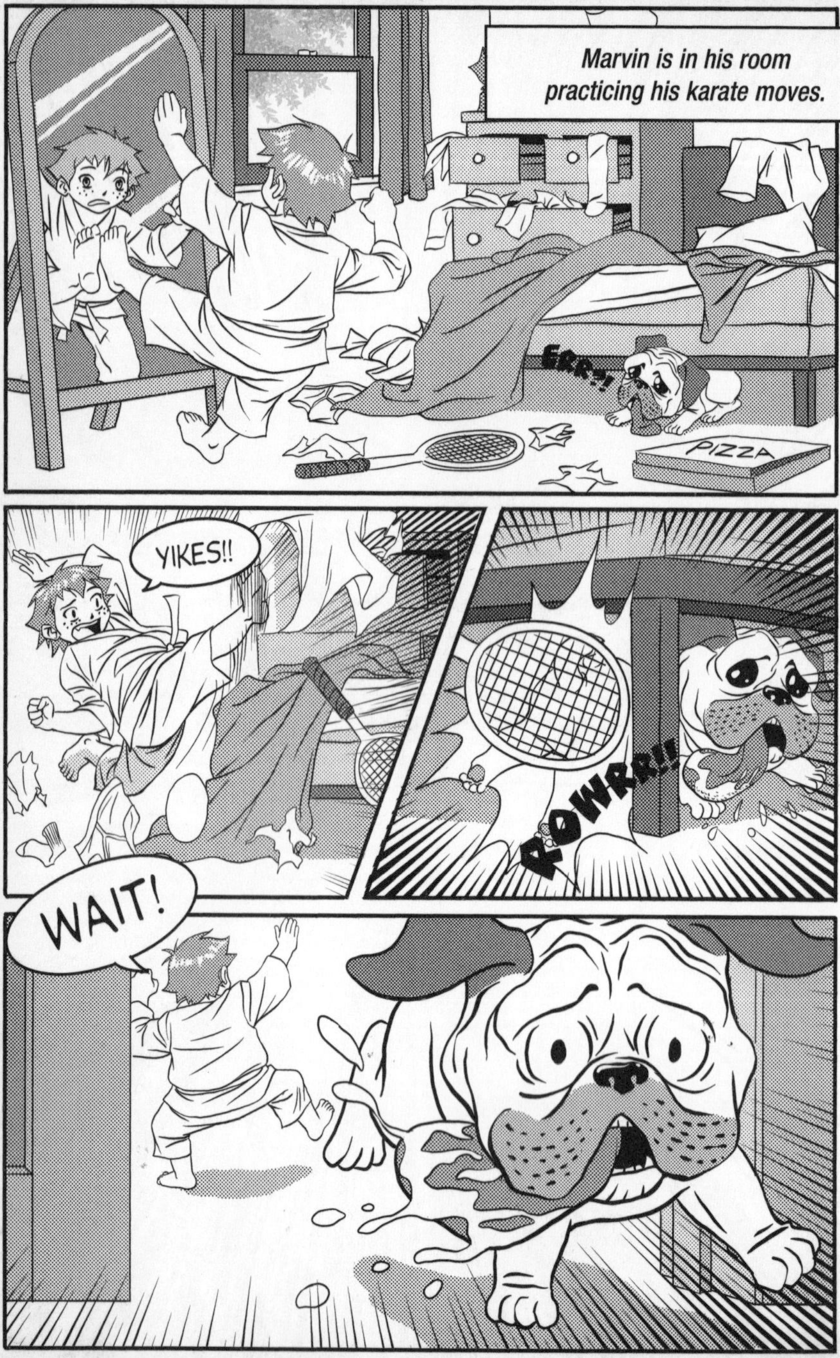

Marvin is in his room practicing his karate moves.
PIZZA
YIKES!!
ROWRR!!
WAIT!

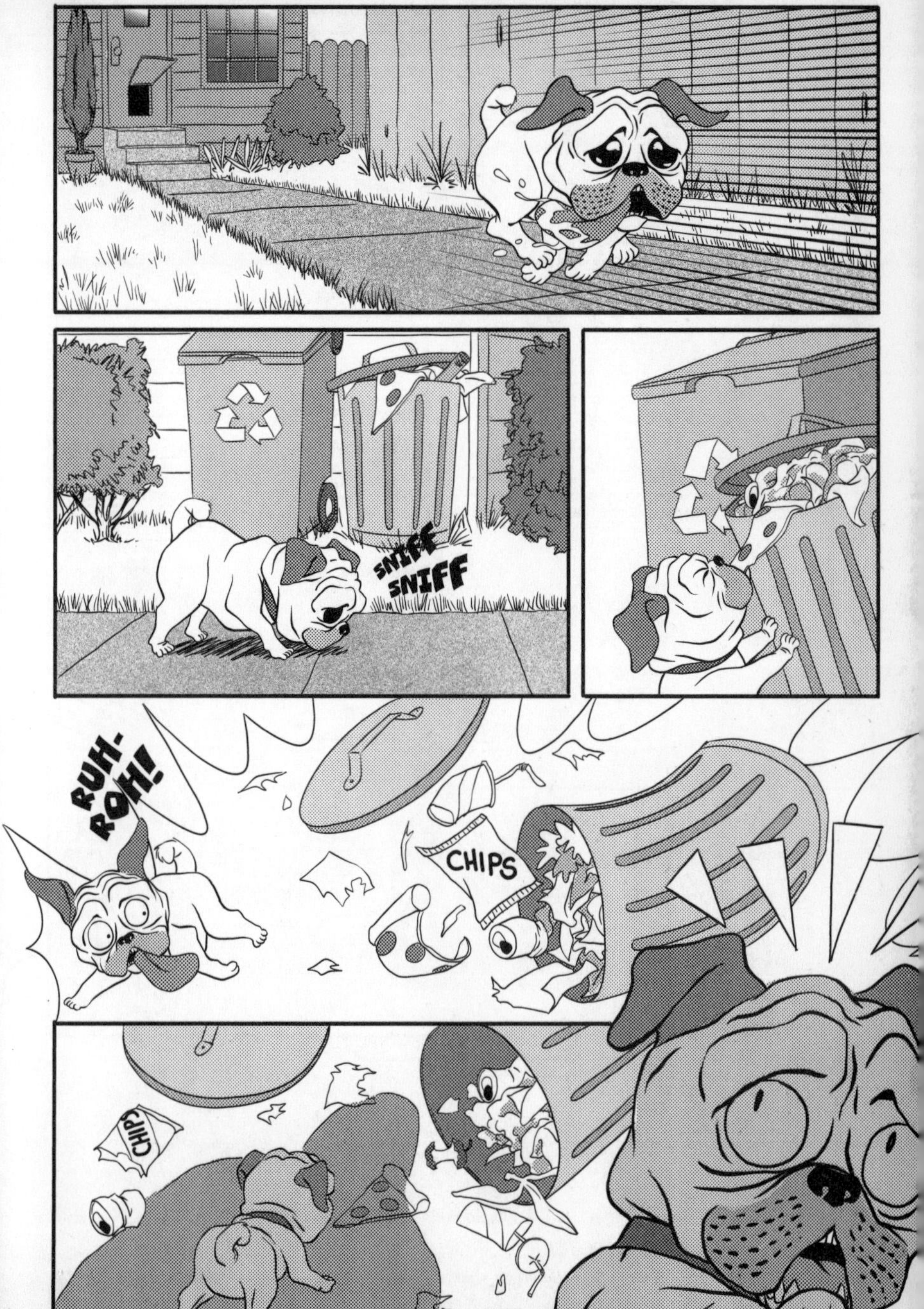
SNIFF
SNIFF
RUH-
ROH!
CHIPS
CHIPS

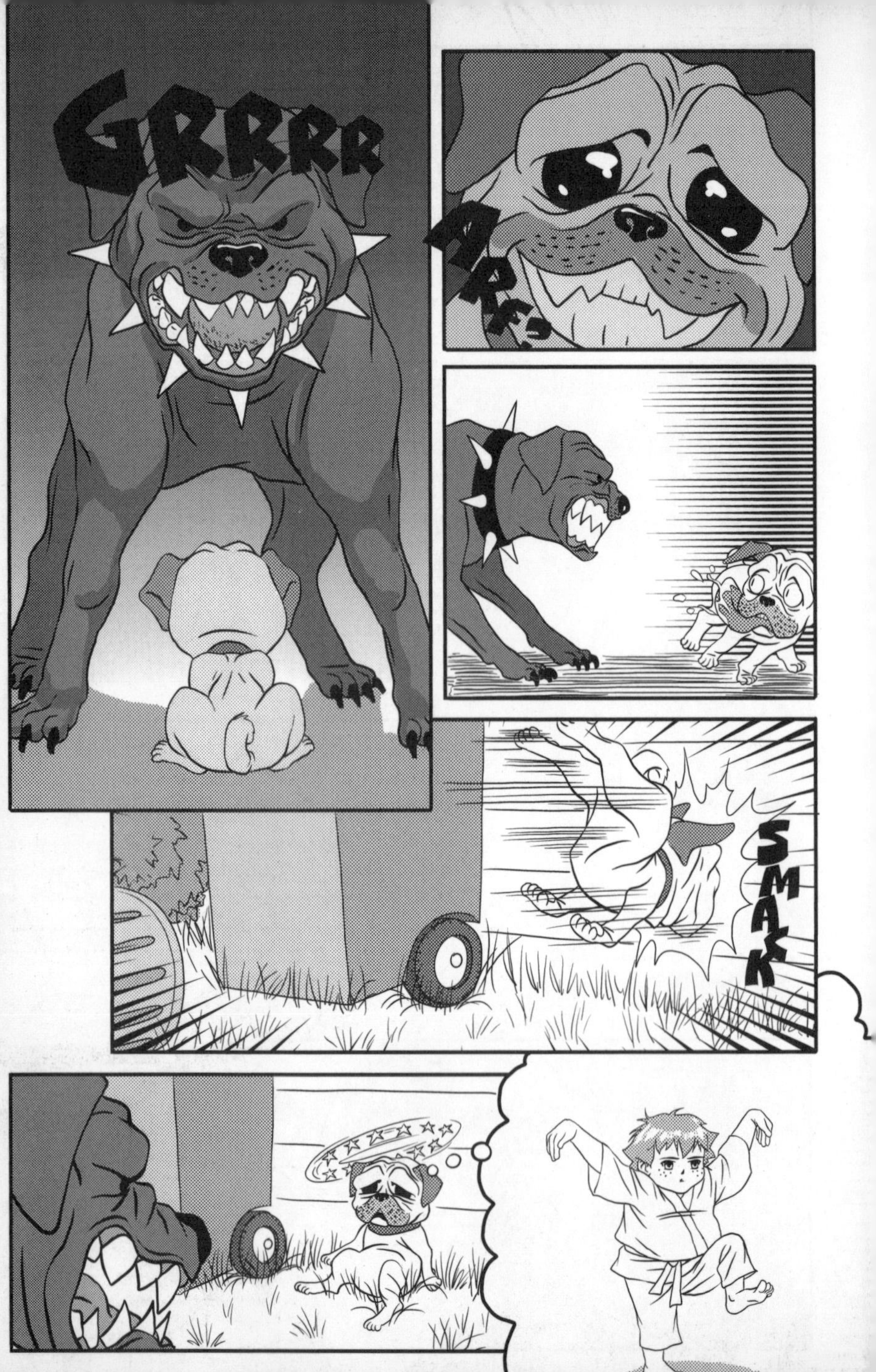
GRRRR
ARF?
SMAK

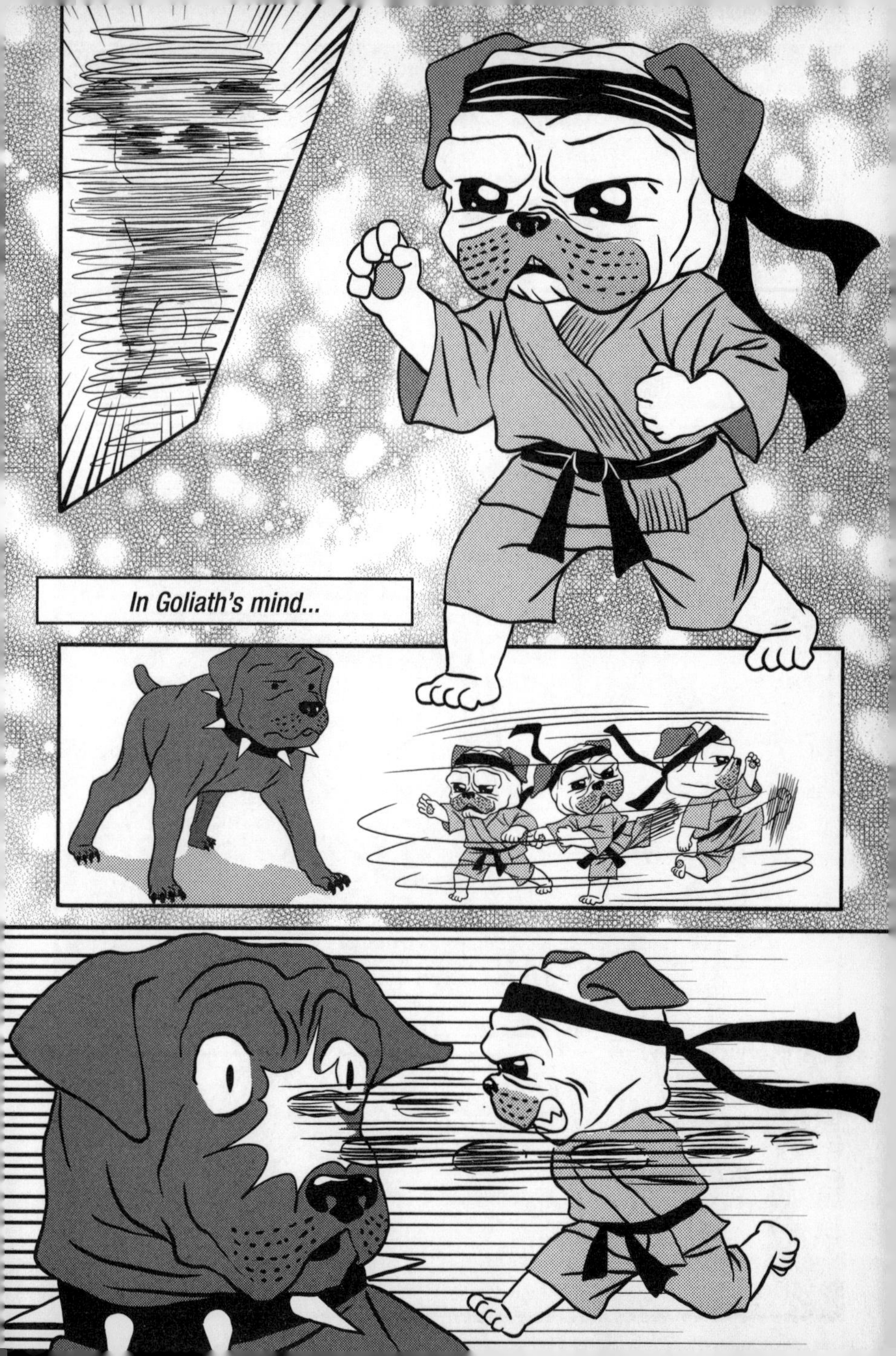
In Goliath's mind...

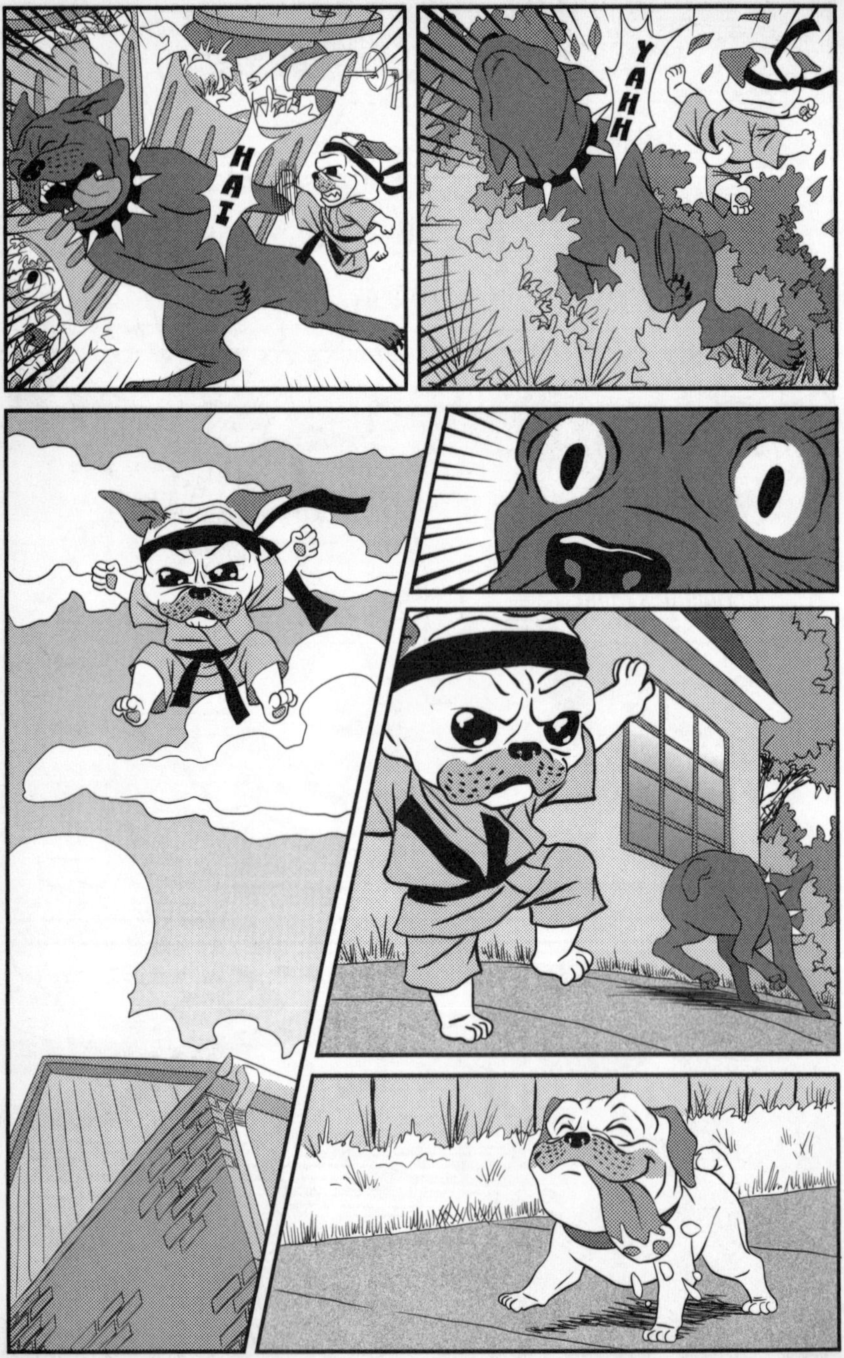
HAI
YAHH

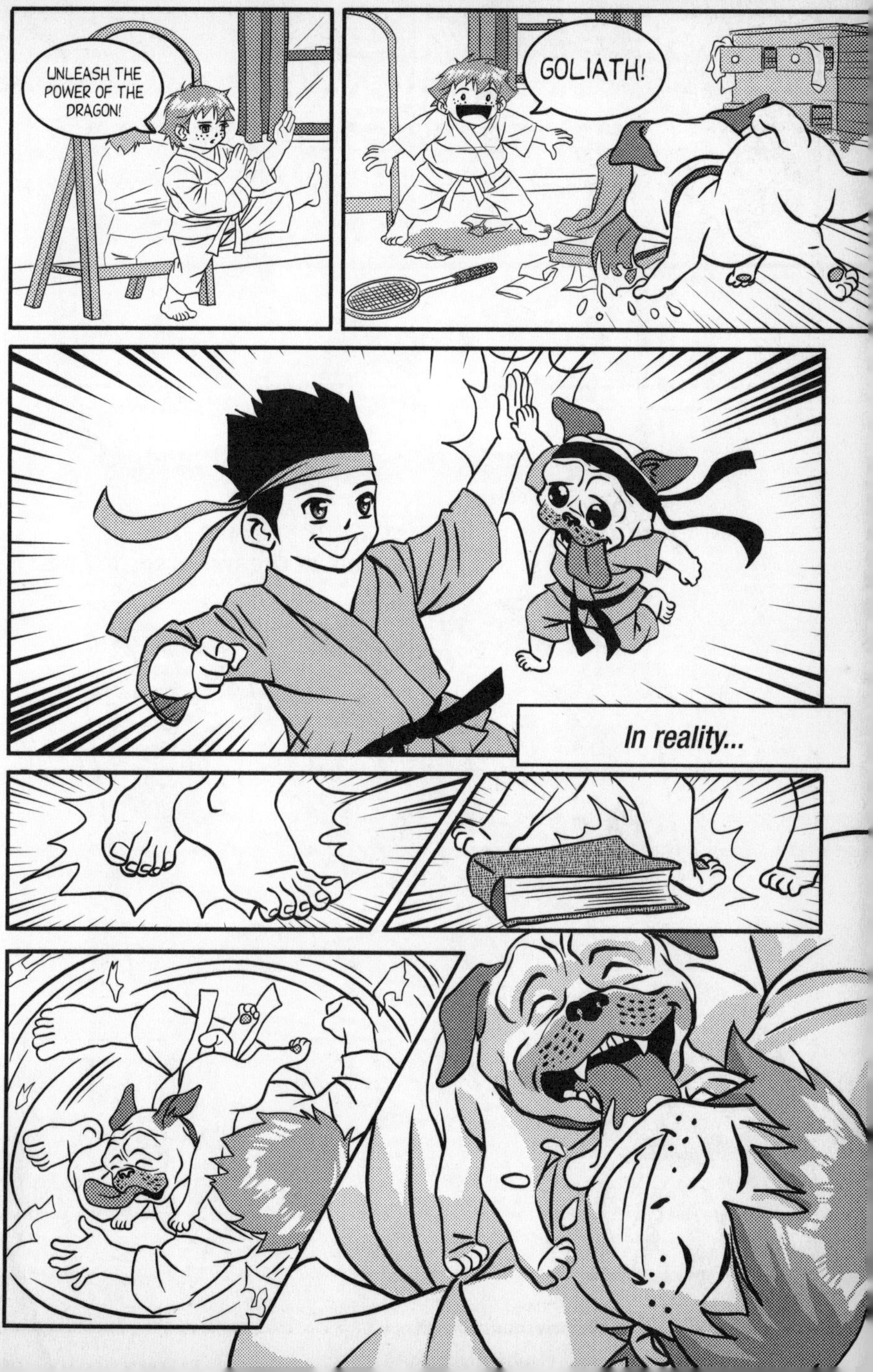
UNLEASH THE POWER OF THE DRAGON!
GOLIATH!
In reality...